WHAT REVIEWERS ARE SAYING ABOUT
SHE-WOLF

"A young Ukrainian woman is determined to get to the bottom of her beloved grandparents' suspicious deaths in Moss' thriller....An auspicious revenge tale with an unconventional heroine."

— *Kirkus Reviews*

"She-Wolf is a gut-punch of a thriller. Complex characters caught up in a story of survival, revenge, and family. Not for the faint of heart!"

— Jonathan Maberry, *New York Times* bestselling author of *Rot & Ruin and V-Wars*

"This story really captured my imagination. I found myself turning page after page. The author clearly did extensive research in the culture, language, and location of the story. He did something that is the hallmark of great writing. He made the reader care deeply about the main character."

— Thomas H Murray, Author of *The Adventures of Nuno and Figo: The Strange Journey of Two Unlikely Friends*

SHE-WOLF

She doesn't hide. She hunts.

a novel

francis moss

SHE-WOLF: SHE DOESN'T HIDE. SHE HUNTS. by Francis Moss

Copyright © 2022 by Francis Moss
www.francismoss.com

First Edition

Published by Encelia Press in the United States of America

This is a work of fiction. Names, places, characters, and incidents are either the product of the author's imagination or are used fictitiously, and any resemblance to actual persons, living or dead, business establishments, events, or locales is entirely coincidental. We assume no liability for errors, inaccuracies, omissions or any inconsistency therein.

Cover design by Jana Rade

Author services by Pedernales Publishing, LLC.
www.pedernalespublishing.com

Library of Congress Control Number: 2021925626

ISBN: Paperback edition   978-1-7327910-3-9
ISBN: Digital edition   978-1-7327910-4-6
ISBN: Hardcover edition   978-1-7327910-5-3

Printed in the United States of America

xx-v10

To Phyllis...thanks for putting up with me.

ACKNOWLEDGEMENTS

Thanks especially to my wife Phyllis, whose patience with me ("Not now, I'm writing!") and critical eye helped make my writing as good as I can make it.

Thanks to Laura Garwood & Kristen Hall-Geisler of Indigo Editing, whose sympathetic and thoughtful responses guided me in shaping my storytelling and character-making.

Thanks to Jose Ramirez at Pedernales Publishing, who held my sweaty hand on the path to this and my other books, and who gently steered me in the right direction when I wanted to go left (I'm left-handed; it's a habit).

Thanks to Brian Schwartz of Self-Publish.org, who told me that everything I thought I knew about marketing my books was just the beginning.

Thanks to my readers and the members of the Desert Writers Guild, all of whom were helpful in more ways than I can count.

To friends and fellow writers, Jean-Paul Garnier, Rich Soos, Brent Harris and others I've left out who will be sure to tell me that I forgot to mention them. Apologies.

CONTENTS

PART ONE: NOW

CHAPTER 1

I woke up in pitch darkness to the sound of an engine and the smell of exhaust. My head hurt where someone had hit me. We went over a bump, and a dim red light flashed. I was in the trunk of a car. My wrists and ankles were tied. I felt something wet and warm running down my head and onto my cheek. Blood. Mine.

I am Deborah Sokolov. I am not dying today.

I twisted around, trying to find something sharp to cut myself free. Another bump, another brake light, and I saw a familiar green blanket stuffed in a corner. I wiggled forward to put my face in it. The blanket smelled of cigars. I was in Grandpa's old Buick.

As I reached behind me to pry up the thin board covering the spare tire, the car came to a stop and I slid forward. A car door, two car doors slammed. The trunk lid opened. I squinted at the flashlight shining in my eyes. Two shadowy figures hovered above me.

"*My ub´yem yeye seychas,*" a gruff voice said in Russian. In Ukrainian, "kill her" is "*vbyy yiyi.*" Different spelling, but it sounds exactly like the Russian.

"*Nyet. My podozhdem,*" a higher-pitched voice replied.

Then, in English with a Russian accent: "No. He needs to see her."

The flashlight went out. Two pairs of hands pulled me from the trunk and dropped me onto planks. I was on the boardwalk. The Ferris wheel was still. Behind me was Café Volna, closed and dark. A tiny breeze blew the smell of cooking oil and fish to me. A sliver of the setting moon hung above the water behind Steeplechase Pier, far away down the broad beach.

The two Russians—one tall and skinny, the other short and fat—picked me up and carried me toward the sand. They were wearing black suits, but I'd seen them before in police uniforms. I struggled and fought, trying to get free. The fat one dropped my feet, leaned over, and smacked me with his fist. "Stop it, foolish girl." He hit me where the blood was coming from, and it hurt. He took out a handkerchief and wiped his balding head. "The humidity, Armin. It is *uzhasnyy*, terrible. Even at night."

Armin, the skinny Russian, nodded. "It's the global warming." He bent down, snapped open a switchblade, and cut the ties on my ankles. "She can walk. But," he smiled as he leaned over me and put the knife to my chest, "watch her."

The fat Russian took out a pistol—a silenced Glock 19 with a fifteen-round magazine—and pointed it at me. "Move."

I got to my feet then dropped to my knees, groaning loudly. "My head. It hurts."

"Of course it hurts. I hit you," the fat Russian said. He laughed. "This is the famous killer? I'm not impressed."

Armin gave him a look. "The drug dealer is dead. The man we sent for her? The police found his body. Do not be *glupyy*, Dimitri." I knew that word: it's Russian for "stupid."

Armin yanked me to my feet. "Someone might be awake in one of those apartments," he said, nodding his head toward the buildings along the boardwalk. "Take her over to the benches. He should be here in a few minutes."

We headed down the boardwalk to a covered sitting area, passing a bent metal beach chair with torn green-and-white striped cloth. Fat Dimitri kept poking his Glock into my back. He was too close, and I was pretty sure I could take it from him. But Armin probably had a gun as well as a knife and would shoot me before I could get Dimitri's gun.

Dimitri shoved me down on a bench under the metal awning. He sat down facing me and wiped his face. He glanced at Armin. "Where is he?"

Armin shrugged. "Give me your phone."

"I left it in our car," Dimitri answered.

Armin made a *fuff* noise. "Why did you leave it there? That was stupid."

"And where is your phone, Armin?"

Armin made a *fuff* noise again then headed back to the boardwalk. A black Mercedes was parked behind Grandpa's Buick.

I bent over double, groaning. "I don't feel good. I think I'm sick."

"It will pass," Dimitri said. He sat down heavily on the bench across from me, pointing the Glock in my general direction. Over his shoulder, I saw the inside light in the Mercedes go off and Armin stepping off the boardwalk and walking back to us across the sand. I had maybe five seconds.

Someone really, really wants me dead. *But I am Deborah Sokolov. I am not dying today.*

PART TWO: THEN

CHAPTER 2

In Ukrainian, "grandfather" is "*didus,*" pronounced "deedooz." "Grandmother" is "*babusya,*" pronounced "bahboosyah." My brother Ethan and I had lived with our grandparents since I was two, when our parents were killed in an auto accident. Grandma Nadiya and Grandpa Viktor became our parents. Ethan, who was six when Mom and Dad died, sometimes talked about them. But to me they were just fuzzy photos in Grandma's album, faint memories of warmth, of being held, of candles on a birthday cake, of laughter—like something in a commercial or a photo in store-bought frame.

Ethan and I lived with *Didus* and *Babusya* in a two-story white house with green trim and roses in the tiny front yard, a cracked cement walkway leading up to the porch's creaky wooden steps, a metal railing that Grandpa had installed when Grandma started to get a little wobbly. Our house was on Second Street in a part of Brooklyn called Brighton Beach, which everyone I knew called *Malen´ka Odesa*, Little Odessa.

Ukrainians celebrated Christmas, called *Rizdvo*, on January 7, because, according to Grandma, Eastern Orthodox Catholics observed holidays by the Julian calendar. I think they just wanted to be different from everyone else. January 6, Christmas Eve, was a big deal. Family, neighbors, and friends crowded into our little house on Brighton 2nd Street, bringing borscht, stuffed salmon, potatoes, peas, twisted bread that my friend Rose said was just like the Jewish bread challah. The grownups ate and argued while my brother Ethan and I hurried to finish eating so we could get out of the room.

During the holidays, while other houses on our block had Hondas and Chevrolets parked in front, the street in front of our grandparents' house was filled with Mercedes, Caddies, Humvees, and Teslas. It had always been that way. I thought it was normal. Except for the fancy cars, we were just like the other people on the block. Grandpa's car was an old green Buick.

I first realized just how different we were when Ethan was in eighth grade. As I walked home from school and opened the squeaky front gate, my brother hurried by, bumping me and covering his face.

"Watch it, stupid!" I said. Ethan didn't answer. He hurried up the wooden steps into the house, stumbling on the top stair.

I ran up the front steps after him and into the house. Ethan's feet thudded up the inside stairs as Grandma came out of the kitchen, wiping her hands on her apron.

"Ah *vnuchko, vnuk*," she said, smiling as she always did. She ran her hand over her thick gray hair pulled back in a bun, the only way I'd ever seen her wear it. "How was your school today?"

"*Tse bulo dobre, Babusya*. It was good, Grandma." I replied, my part of our daily ritual. I heard Ethan's bedroom door slam. Grandma frowned. Ethan was supposed to be here for the ritual. For at least five minutes each day, we told her what we had learned and how our friends and miscellaneous second and third cousins were doing.

Grandma asked, "What is wrong with your brother?"

"I don't know. I'll find out," I said and hurried up the stairs two at a time. I knocked on his door. "Hey, Ethan. Wassup?" No answer. I knocked again. "Open the door."

"Go away!" he said. I knocked a few more times and tried to open the door, but it was locked. Being the bratty little sister that I was, I kept pounding on the door until he opened it. Ethan had a bloody lip and a red bruise on his cheek. "I said go away!" he yelled at me, slamming the door shut.

"You got into a fight! And I bet you lost!" I said to the door. I went down to the kitchen, where Grandma was at the old iron-and-porcelain stove, stirring a pot that smelled of cabbage. In our house you either liked cabbage or you went hungry. I told her about Ethan.

"Viktor will talk to him," she said, taking a sip from the spoon.

Grandpa Viktor was a bookkeeper at East-West Imports, the company owned by Teodor Kosenko, Uncle Teddy to me. He wasn't really my uncle, just another member of our extended Ukrainian family. By the time I was eight or ten, I'd figured out that Uncle Teddy wasn't my uncle, and that East-West Imports wasn't a regular company but a front for the *orhanizatsiyi*, the Ukrainian Mafia. Stories circulated about insurance fraud, fake designer clothes, smuggled immigrants, and welfare and Medicare scams. Grandpa and Grandma never talked about those things. Grandpa wasn't a mobster. He was a mobster's bookkeeper.

Grandpa usually got home around five, but Grandma must have called him, because he came home early that afternoon. I was in the living room doing geometry homework.

The front door opened. I got up, ran into the hall, and leaped up on Grandpa, who was just putting down his plastic briefcase.

I smelled the odor of shaving cream and Tic Tacs. He used the little mints to hide the smell of the cigars, which, despite Grandma's warning, he occasionally smoked.

He hugged me with his big strong arms, and I ruffled his thick gray hair. He smiled, deepening the wrinkles around his gray eyes, then put me down.

"Ethan got beat up," I said, tattler that I was.

"I know, Deborah."

"Want to see my homework?" I asked.

"Later, *zaichik*," he said and walked up the stairs to Ethan's room.

I tiptoed up the stairs to see the door open and Grandpa going in, closing it behind him. I put my ear to the door, but I could only hear Grandpa's growly voice.

Dinner was all weird because Ethan just poked at the food on his plate, Grandma and Grandpa exchanged looks. No one talked.

As we finished eating (except Ethan), the doorbell rang. I jumped up. "I'll get it." Grandma reached for my hand, but I was too fast. I ran to the door and opened it.

A red-faced, curly-haired man stood there with a red-faced, curly-haired kid of about thirteen. Behind them, a black Lincoln was parked in front of the house. Voly, one of Uncle Teddy's associates, leaned against it. Voly was

Volodymyr, one of Uncle Teddy's soldiers, my friend and oc-casional babysitter since I could remember. Tattoos climbed up his neck above his shirt collar and onto his shaved head. He raised a hand to wave at me.

Grandpa came to the door, nudging me out of the way. "Come in, come in."

I ran ahead of them into the living room and plopped myself down on the couch. That lasted for three seconds until Grandma came in, glared at me, then nodded to the stairs. I got the message. I stomped into the hallway and up the stairs, sitting down on the top step. Grandpa shook the man's hand, and the three of them went into the living room.

Grandma appeared at the bottom of the stairs. She looked at me, shook her head, raised her left eyebrow, and with her thumb pointed to my room. One raised eyebrow meant "Do it!" I went to my room and noisily shut the door. I waited a minute then tiptoed back to the head of the stairs. I crept a couple of steps down, careful to avoid the creaking fifth and six steps and Grandma's wrath.

I sat on the stairs and watched through the banister as Grandpa gestured to the sagging maroon couch. "Sit, please." They sat.

Grandma took Ethan's arm and led him into the living room, where he stood looking down at the floor.

Grandpa said, "Mr. Cogosin. I appreciate your coming over to deal with this. Young boys can be…thoughtless."

The dad said in a squeaky voice, "Thank you for…for the opportunity."

"And this is your son Grigori?"

"*Da…*" He cleared his throat. "*Moy syn i ya—*"

"English, please. And let your son speak."

The kid offered another throat clearing and said in a higher voice, "Er, I'm sorry, Ethan."

"For what, Grigori?" Grandpa asked.

"For punching you in the face."

"And...?" his dad prompted.

"For calling you a *kogoot*."

I knew that word. Russian kids in our neighborhood would yell it at us Ukrainians and spit. I had no clue what it meant.

Grandpa said, "I think we must leave behind the differences between Russians and Ukrainians. Here we are all Americans. Do you agree?"

The dad and the kid nodded.

"Very good. Now, Ethan, Grigori, shake hands. I am sure this will not happen again. Volodymyr will take you home," he said to our visitors.

And that's how I began to learn that we were different. By the time I got to high school, I learned that Carol and Angie, my girlfriends, had known for a while what kind of business my grandfather worked for. They didn't care.

❧❧❧

One day at school, Rick, a sprinter who was tall and skinny like me, with big blue eyes, joined me in the hallway after seventh period. As we walked to the entrance, we talked about music, cross-country versus the hundred-meter dash, and unimportant stuff. I think he was cranking up the nerve to ask me out. Then, outside the school, he saw Voly waiting for me, leaning against a Hummer, his giant arms folded. That was the last time for Rick.

CHAPTER

I thought I needed new running shoes. The heat from the pavement on Fifth Street made my feet hurt, and I wanted to get into the park to run on the grass next to the path. Sweat soaked my headband and ran down my cheeks. Ahead of me, Brianna, who'd always be the fastest, no matter how hard I tried, was cruising, holding her earbuds, listening to her boring music. The six of us on the Millennium Brooklyn High cross-country team crossed Prospect Park West without waiting for the signal, dodging cars and bicycles. Coach Robbins would be pissed.

It was cooler under the trees. I felt the breeze drying my sweat, and I picked up my pace. No leg cramps today, I promised myself. I was finally finding my pace—not trying to beat Brianna, just trying to keep my rhythm. It was like Coach Robbins said: find the center of myself, where I could run all day. I thought about Pheidippides, the Greek man who ran from Marathon to Athens to announce the Persian defeat, then collapsed and died. He probably should have hydrated.

Down to the lake and around, my leg muscles were saying, "We're going to cramp, we're going to cramp," no matter how much I told them to stop it.

The breezes off the lake felt good. I closed the distance between me and Brianna, and I had nearly caught up to her as we headed to West Drive and the exit. Just as I was thinking, *Maybe I can beat her*, she stepped up her pace and left me behind again.

CHAPTER 4

The day after my seventeenth birthday, I came home from school, tossed my backpack on the chair in the hall—which Grandma was sure to tell me about—and headed for the kitchen to grab something to eat. As I walked by Grandpa's office, I saw that the door, which was usually shut, was open. A small, gray metal box, its lid closed, was on his desk. Next to it was a smaller black box, its lid open.

I stopped at the door for a second, then I went in. Inside the black box was a tiny wire brush, some cloth squares, and a metal rod. I opened the gray box. A pistol nestled in cloth, small and black and shiny like a toy, was in it. I reached for it, then stopped. I closed the box, then opened it again and picked up the pistol. It was heavy, too heavy for a toy; the dark wood handle, with a raised pattern of tiny diamond-shaped bumps, fit into my hand. A star with a T inside it was stamped in the metal above the handle.

With my thumb, I pulled the notched lever on top—a hammer, I remembered from somewhere—and the cylinder turned with a click. I pulled the hammer again, and it went back into its slot. The pistol smelled of oil and something else—a story maybe.

I looked into the barrel, which was fairly stupid, but at least I knew not to put my finger on the trigger. Under the barrel was a small black rod. I pulled it, and the cylinder swung out from the side on a little hinge. It had seven empty holes for bullets. I pushed the cylinder back in. I aimed at the lamp by the window and pulled the trigger. The hammer went back, the cylinder turned, and click! The hammer went down.

In my mind, the lamp exploded. Click! The phone on the desk shattered and fell off. Click! The ticking pendulum clock on the wall splintered into pieces. Click! The bearded, creepy-looking Ukrainian ancestor in an old, framed photo on the side table got an imaginary hole in in his head. I shot at things and changed them, made them go away. I felt something: not scared, something else, something new. I aimed at the little shelf behind Grandpa's desk and took out the old books one by one, click click click.

I turned and there was Grandpa at the door watching me with wide eyes. "I'm sorry, *Didus*," I began. "I didn't—" I opened the box to put the gun back, but I was clumsy. The pistol fell to the desk. "Oops. Sorry. I'll—"

"Hush." Grandpa came over and picked up the pistol. He nodded to the worn red leather chair behind me. "Sit, Deborah."

I sat. He knelt in front of me, and his knees cracked. The pendulum clock ticked. A car with a broken muffler drove down our street. He looked at me for what felt like two minutes but was maybe a few seconds. I looked away, reading the Ukrainian book titles on the shelf. I waited for him to yell at me, but Grandpa was not Grandma.

"This is my fault. I was cleaning it and forgot to put it

away," Grandpa said. He held up the gun. "But you must never touch this again without my permission."

I nodded. I exhaled. Grandpa put the gun into the gray metal box, closed and locked it with a key, opened a drawer in his desk, and put both boxes in it. "Go. Do your homework. Nadiya will be asking about it."

I turned at the door. "Teach me how to shoot, Grandpa."

He shook his head. "No. Not for girls. Not for you."

I grabbed my backpack and went upstairs to my room. I started on the chapter of the book we were reading in English class. But the smell of gun oil and the feeling of the gun, the tiny diamond-shaped bumps on the handle, were a memory on my hands.

&c&c&c

The next day, I sat in the living room waiting for Grandpa to get home. Not to jump on him anymore—I was too old for that.

Grandpa came in, hung his old leather jacket on the coat rack, then turned to see me. He seemed surprised. "Do you want something, Deborah?"

I took a deep breath. "I want to learn how to shoot," I said.

He frowned. "I told you. No."

"Please, Grandpa? Teach me."

"Why?"

It wasn't possible to look away from Grandpa's gray eyes. "I want to learn." I smiled. "It's something we can do together."

That was pretty lame, but it made him think. He curled his lip. "Why?" he asked again.

"I...I don't know."

"Your grandmother would not approve."

The words *We don't have to tell her* came to me, but that would have been dumb. Grandpa turned and walked into his office. I followed him. He put his bent and scratched plastic briefcase on his desk and waved his hand. "I have things to take care of. Go do your homework."

My homework included googling "women and shooting."

࿊ ࿊ ࿊

I was again waiting for Grandpa to come home, again sitting in the living room next to Grandpa's office. He sighed. "I already said no."

I whipped out the paper I'd printed from Wikipedia and showed it to him. "Look, Grandpa. Kim Rhode. She won her first shooting medal at age thirteen. And she won an Olympic medal at age seventeen! My age!" I had three other pages ready, just in case.

Grandpa glanced at the paper then back at me. "Why is this so important to you?"

I'd been asking myself the same question for three days. All I knew is that when I held Grandpa's pistol and pretended to shoot at things, it was like the feeling I had in sixth grade when I started running cross-country. My body, which I'd always kind of hated—too skinny, too clumsy—began to work for me, not against me. I'd started on the dirt track at school, the coach telling me, "Don't overdo it, Deborah. One lap." Four laps later I was breathing fast, but my legs wanted to do more. The coach had to grab my arm to stop me. He smiled. "I think you're a runner."

I couldn't tell Grandpa all that. "I want to find out what I can do, Grandpa. Something besides cross-country." I stood up and went to the window overlooking our tiny front yard. "And…I don't know…something…When I held your pistol, I thought I could be good at it. Like Kim Rhode."

Grandpa came to stand next to me. I turned to look at him. His face was sad. He sighed again, heavily. "I will talk to Nadiya. We will see."

"Yes!" I yelled and hugged him. "Thank you, thank you." Grandpa hugged me back but not so happily. He wasn't sharing my joy, probably imagining how his conversation with Grandma would go.

I went up to my room to browse some more about guns and shooting. I read about a Ukrainian, Lyudmila Pavlichenko, the most famous woman sniper in World War II. She was credited with 309 kills fighting the Nazis and was the first Soviet soldier invited to the White House to meet President Roosevelt. Annie Oakley could split a playing card edge-on at 90 feet with her .22 rifle.

A little later, I heard Grandma and Grandpa talking outside in the backyard. I looked out the window. They were sitting in their old plastic lawn chairs, arguing. Grandma was angry: "*Ty dozvolyv yiy znyaty pistolet!*" I understood *pistolet*. She was pissed because Grandpa had told her what I wanted to do.

êêê

After a tense and silent dinner, I went into the kitchen to help Grandma with the dishes. I usually (OK, *always*) had to be asked, so she gave me the eye. "Maybe you want something, *vnuchka*. A new computer?"

A deep breath. "I don't want you to fight with Grandpa. About him teaching me how to shoot."

Grandma scrubbed the dinner plate extra hard. I was expecting an argument—"not for little girls"—which I'd been hearing since I begged for my first two-wheeler when I was six and knew I'd hear from her when I was twenty-six. Instead, she handed me the well-scrubbed plate to rinse, looked at me, and sighed.

"It's more complicated than you know, Deborah."

"Explain it to me then."

Grandma shook her head. "That is for Viktor. I know you are stubborn, and you want your own way in things. But you are not careless. I do not worry that you will hurt yourself or others, but—" She waved it away. "Your grandfather will talk to you." She wiped her hands on her apron and grabbed me by the shoulders, turning me to face her. "Tell me. Why is this so important?"

"I think I might be good at it. Really good."

Grandma laughed. "You are good at lots of things, Deborah. What are you talking about?"

"No. I'm just OK at things. Ethan has always gotten better grades, Brianna is faster than me on cross-country…"

Grandma shook her head and picked up an already-clean plate, scrubbing hard on it. I thought her worry might have something to do with our gangster-adjacent family. But I was never going to be a gangster. "Do you know about Lyudmila Pavlichenko?" I asked.

Grandma smiled for the first time. "Every Ukrainian knows about Lyudmila. In Kyiv there is a statue of her."

"If I practice, maybe I can compete on a pistol team when I go to college. A woman on the US Olympics pistol team—"

Grandma waved her hand. "Enough. Finish the dishes. And make sure you dry them well." She started putting dishes and utensils back in the cabinets and drawers.

As I dried the last teacup, Grandma said, "Viktor loves you very much. He would not do something that was wrong for you." Then she wiped her hands on her apron and hugged me. Grandma usually saved hugs for birthdays and good report cards; this was unusual. She pulled away. "Your stupid cat is meowing on the porch. Go feed it."

Dobby was a skinny, orange feral cat with white on her chin and feet, completely lacking in charm or manners. She'd been a part-time resident and regular visitor since I was in tenth grade. Dobby would never let anyone touch her but was always expecting bowls of food and water on our back porch steps. Grandma was sure she was rabid, and if she scratched or bit me, I would die horribly.

Dobby and I had developed an edgy friendship. She'd let me sit on the steps while she ate, looking up at me every few seconds to make sure I wouldn't do something stupid, like try to pet her. She'd kind of growl-meow and show her teeth, as if to say, "I'm tough. Don't mess with me." She reminded me a little of Grandma.

I was getting ready for bed when there was a knock on my bedroom door. Grandpa's knock. I opened the door, and he stood there for a minute just looking at me. I was about to say something when he said, "After we take your grandmother to church tomorrow, we will go to the warehouse. We will see."

෯෯෯

Every Sunday, Grandma Nadiya went to the Ukrainian Saint Nicholas Orthodox Church on Nineteenth Street. Grandpa took her and picked her up, but he would never go inside. By now they'd established a grudging truce on the religious issue. When we were younger, Grandma would drag Ethan and me to church until we started complaining ("It's all old people!" "I can't understand anything!" "It smells funny!"). She finally gave up, muttering darkly under her breath about "*hrikh i spokusa*," which means sin and temptation.

It was still dark when I woke up Sunday. I stared at the patterns in the ceiling of my room, remembering the feel of the gun in my hand, remembering that today Grandpa Viktor was going to teach me how to shoot. I couldn't get back to sleep, so I got up, showered, brushed my teeth, got dressed, and went downstairs to wait.

After breakfast, I got into the back seat of our old Buick, and Grandma got in the front. Grandpa started the car and backed out of the driveway. Grandma turned to me. "Come to church, Deborah."

I shook my head. "Grandpa and me are—"

"We are going to my office," Grandpa interrupted. "I have work to do. Deborah wants to come."

Grandma grunted. She knew where we were going, but we were not supposed to talk about it.

We dropped Grandma off at the church, then went to East-West Imports. I'd been there before. It was on the East River in an old red brick warehouse with cracked cement floors that smelled of fish and chemicals. Grandpa's desk was in the office upstairs, with a dirty window that looked across the river to Governor's Island and Manhattan.

That morning we didn't go upstairs. I followed Grandpa, who was carrying his plastic briefcase, to a narrow cement stairway heading down under the building. A rusty iron stair rail on one wall was flaking off green paint. At the bottom was a locked metal door. Grandpa pulled his keys out of his pocket and unlocked it.

We went in. He punched in 0-4-1-0 on the alarm box— the anniversary of his and Grandma's wedding—then flipped a switch on the wall. Fluorescent lights crackled and stuttered to life. We were in a long, narrow, windowless brick-walled room. Bundled stacks of newspapers were piled up to the ceiling at one end; at the other end were three small tables and some chairs. I shivered, although it wasn't that cold. The room had a faint smell, like Grandpa's gun.

Grandpa put his briefcase on one of the tables, opened it, and took out the cleaning kit, the gun, and a box of bullets. I shivered again. The only sound was the faint fizzing from the lights above.

Grandpa held the gun out. I reached for it, but he closed his big hand over it. "Rule number one: a gun is always loaded unless you check it for sure." He opened the cylinder so I could see that the gun was empty, then he closed it with a click. "Rule number two: never point this at anything you do not intend to shoot." I nodded.

"It is a Russian gun, a Nagant, very old." I reached for it again, but he pushed my hand away and pointed at the parts. "This is the grip, this is the cylinder, this is the trigger, this is the hammer, these are the sights." Finally, he handed to pistol to me, grip first, barrel pointing down.

Grandpa showed me how to aim by looking at the front sight on the barrel through the grooved rear sight. He showed me the correct stance: left hand cupping my right hand as I aimed, feet slightly apart. He took the gun and put in on the table, then opened the box of bullets that said "7.62 mm x 39," whatever that meant. In the box were brass and copper shells all standing in rows. He handed the gun to me grip-first. "Load it."

I opened the cylinder and took a bullet from the box. It slipped from my shaky fingers and fell to the floor. Grandpa tried not to smile. I picked it up and stuck it into the hole in the cylinder, followed by the next six, not dropping even one. I closed the cylinder and put the gun on the table, smiling proudly. I stopped smiling when Grandpa turned the gun so it wasn't pointing at his leg.

He turned to face the pile of newspapers and pointed. "You are shooting that way," he said. "Face your target, then turn halfway. Both eyes open, elbows loose, left hand over your right. The pistol will kick in your hand, but it is a small caliber, so not so much." He showed me his stance, and it looked like something he knew well.

Grandpa handed me the pistol, and I stood in what I hoped was the correct stance. "Take a breath, let it out, aim, and fire."

I squinted down the barrel, took a breath, my finger on the trigger. Grandpa put his hand over mine, pushing my arms down. "Keep your arms straight, but don't lock your elbows. Breathe, relax, squeeze the trigger. Do not pull it."

I raised my arms, looking through the groove at the front sight. I breathed, relaxed maybe a little, and squeezed the trigger. I heard a POP! My hands, my arms tingled. I breathed in, smelling the odor of gunpowder. It was like the feeling I'd had in Grandpa's office when I first held the pistol.

I put the gun on the table, remembering not to point it at Grandpa, then went down to the stacks of newspapers. As I got closer, I saw there were dozens, maybe hundreds of holes in them. I couldn't tell which hole my bullet had made.

I turned back to Grandpa. "I want to shoot at targets," I said.

He laughed. "One round she fires." He shook his head. "Next time. For now, get used to the feel of the gun."

I shot at newspapers until the box of bullets was empty and my arms got tired. Then Grandpa showed me how to clean the pistol. I never liked to clean anything (Grandma used to dump my overflowing laundry basket on my bed as a hint). But I liked scrubbing the inside of the cylinders and the barrel with the little brush, wiping the outside, and smelling the odor of gun oil.

Afterward Grandpa and I washed our hands at the rusty sink. "To clean off the gunpowder residue," he said. Then it was time to pick up Grandma Nadiya.

☙☙☙

We went shooting at the warehouse for the next three Sundays. I was getting better at it. I thought about bragging to Ethan, but he was in his senior year at Princeton and never seemed to care much about what I was doing anyway.

One Sunday, after we'd dropped off Grandma at church, I asked if she was OK with my new thing.

"OK? Maybe not. But she has accepted it, in her way," Grandpa said.

I was getting really good. Grandpa, never one to give compliments, nodded approvingly as I learned shot groupings, adjusting for wind deflection, and most of all, gun safety.

I got a little obsessive about the whole shooting thing. I browsed gunmaker websites and studied calibers, laser sights, Glocks, Rugers, Colts, Winchesters, Armalites, gun shows, how many grains in a round, how rifling in the barrel improves accuracy on gun barrels longer than two inches.

Nagant pistols had been made since the nineteenth century, mostly in Russia but also in Poland. Grandpa's gun fired a 7.62 round, but some Nagant owners rechambered theirs for .22-caliber long rifle bullets, meaning they replaced the original barrel. Semiautomatic pistols were faster and held more rounds, but the cheap, poorly made ones were prone to jamming. "Too many moving parts," Grandpa said. He was pretty old school.

When you're seventeen, you're not the boss of anything. School teachers were my bosses for most of the day, Grandma and Grandpa my bosses when I was home. Shooting on Sundays, when I held the Nagant in my hands, I was the boss. I could see something in Grandpa's eyes when he watched me. I thought it was some Old World, "not for girls" thing. But his smile when I did well seemed a little like pride in his granddaughter. Me, I was taking charge of something.

I asked him one morning, after I'd finished putting about sixty rounds in a half-dozen targets and was carefully cleaning the pistol, "Why do you have a gun, Grandpa?"

I think he'd been expecting the question. He chuckled. "This is America. Everyone has a gun."

I thought there was more to it. "Did you ever shoot anybody?"

He didn't answer. He got up from his chair and walked down to collect the targets pinned to the newspaper stacks. He came back and put one of the targets on the table, pointing to the holes. "Your aim was off here," he said. "Look how scattered this group is. I think you were not breathing correctly."

I wiped the gun oil off the pistol then put it into the cracked leather bag Grandpa used when he carried it in his briefcase. "Did you?"

Grandpa sighed and looked at me. "It was in another life, Deborah. A long time ago. Before you were born."

"I won't tell anyone," I said. "Was it something to do with Uncle Teddy?"

He looked at me sharply. "The less you know about that, the better." He got up and put the gun bag in his plastic briefcase. "Time to pick up your *babusya*."

My questions hung like laundry on our backyard line all the way home. Grandma noticed it as we were pulling into our driveway.

"What is wrong?" She asked.

Grandpa just shook his head. "I have work to do."

Grandma looked over her shoulder sharply at me, then at Grandpa. But she didn't say anything.

CHAPTER 5

I was in fifth period English when a boy came in and handed a note to the teacher, Mr. Cochran. He glanced at it and turned to me. "Deborah, you need to go to the office. Take your stuff." I grabbed my backpack and hurried out.

Grandma sat in the office, loose strands of her gray hair coming out from her usually perfect bun. She clasped and unclasped her hands around her old leather purse. She looked up at me when I came in. "*Vash didus' znakhodyt'sya v likarni*," she said.

"English, Grandma."

"Your grandfather is in hospital," she said.

It was my turn to be scared. "What happened? Was it an accident? Will he be OK?"

Grandma stood up. "We must go."

The Buick was parked in front of the school, its rear end sticking out in traffic. Grandma never drove, and this was why. "Let me drive, Grandma," I said. I had my junior license, and Grandpa took me out to practice after school and on Saturdays.

"No."

We got in, and I closed my eyes for most of the trip,

hearing the occasional squeal of brakes and honking of horns.

"Ethan is coming back from Princeton," Grandma said.

I opened one eye. "Tell me, Grandma. Is Grandpa all right?"

Grandma made a face. "*Durnyy likar.* Stupid doctor. He calls me and says Viktor had 'an episode.' What is an episode?" She leaned over the wheel, honking the horn, and aimed for a pedestrian as if he were the doctor.

Amazingly there was a parking spot on DeKalb in front of the emergency entrance. Grandma put the front wheel up on the curb and scraped the bumper against an innocent little tree on the parkway. We hurried inside.

The hallway was crowded with family. Gray-haired Uncle Teddy was there with his wife, Elena, who had bleached highlights, was chubby, and always wore too much makeup. Twenty-something Olek, with his shiny face, crooked teeth, and a nose that looked like a shark fin, sat next to his parents on the green plastic chairs. Voly stood guard with two grim-looking guys in too-tight suits. Doctors and nurses were making wide detours around them, looking down at their clipboards.

Voly reached out, took my hand, and squeezed it. Uncle Teddy came over to me and Grandma. "I am so sorry, Nadiya," Uncle Teddy said. "Viktor said he felt faint. I drove him here myself."

Aunt Elena gave me a giant hug, saying, "So sorry, Deborah. So sorry."

Olek hugged me, which creeped me out a little, but then he and Uncle Teddy's goons were generally creepy—except for Voly. "I'm sorry for this, Deborah. If you need anything, let me know."

"I want to see him," Grandma said.

The door to the emergency room opened, and a bald guy in a white coat, wearing glasses and a beard, came out. He stopped and stared at our crowd. "Mrs. Sokolov?" Grandma and I went over to him while the rest of family and bodyguards clustered behind us. "I'm Dr. Stein," he said. "Your husband, Mr. Sokolov, had a transient ischemic attack, a little stroke. But he's going to be fine."

Grandma raised her eyebrows, her lips in a thin line. She looked like she was going to have a stroke herself or hit the doctor, but Elena leaned forward and whispered in her ear. Grandma nodded. "I can see him?"

The doctor nodded. "He's resting now, but awake." He looked at us. "Only two in the room at a time, please."

Uncle Teddy took Grandma's arm and started toward the room, but Grandma pulled his arm away. "I go with Deborah."

The room smelled of disinfectant and sickness. Grandpa was raised up a little in the bed. He had tubes attached to his arms and up his nose. He opened his eyes as we came in and smiled. "My two favorite ladies."

Grandma leaned over and kissed him, then I did. "You work too hard, Viktor. Too much headaches," Grandma said. "It is time for you to stop."

"Grandma's right," I said. "You should retire."

Grandpa shrugged. "Maybe. But to do what? Sit around and watch the television? Teo still depends on me. No one else knows how to balance the books, keep track of the invoices."

Grandma pulled over a chair and sat next to the bed, holding Grandpa's hand. I walked to the window and looked out at the afternoon traffic on DeKalb while Grandma and Grandpa argued quietly.

After a while, Grandma got up. "He wants to talk to you," she said, going out.

I went over and sat down in the chair Grandma had vacated, scooting it closer to the bed. Grandpa fumbled around, looking for something. He found the controller, its wire wrapped around the bed's side rail, and pushed the button to raise himself up higher. He held out his hand. I took it, noticing for the first time its age spots, wrinkled skin, and blue veins.

"I think it is time you had answers to your questions." He sighed, his other hand to his chest. "In Kyiv, before your grandmother and I came to this country, I worked for Gennady, Teo's father. And I have worked for Teo for a very long time.

"I...I have done things. Things I am ashamed to have done." He looked out the window for a long minute then turned back to me. "When you and Ethan came to us, I told Teo I would not do those things anymore. He was angry, but because I had been loyal for many years, he agreed. So now I work in the office.

"But before, when I was doing those things, I had a rule, which I never broke. I never did harm to anyone—unless they would do harm to me or my family." Grandpa stopped, closing his eyes and sighing.

I didn't know my mouth was open until Grandpa turned to look at me and pointed at his mouth, almost smiling. This was my second father, my almost only father. He had raised me, and he had killed people. I started to say something, but there were no words.

Grandpa sighed. "I love you and Ethan like you were my children. No, you are my children. I watched you when you were learning to shoot. You are a quick learner. You were confident, sure of yourself, not afraid. Even on that first day, you held the Nagant like it was a part of you." Grandpa put his right hand above my heart. "A part of me was proud of you, but it worried me, and it worried Nadiya too." Grandpa sighed again. He took my hand in both of his, squeezing until it hurt. I didn't pull away. "There is a *vovchytsya,* a she-wolf, inside you, Deborah. I saw her when you were shooting. Promise me. The wolf is dangerous to you, to others. You must promise me to be aware of it. Do not let it out."

I was confused. "What are you talking about, Grandpa?" He was sick and full of drugs.

He shook his head and squeezed my hands even harder. "Promise me. Promise me!"

"I promise, Grandpa," I said, not knowing what I was promising. His grip loosened, and I pulled my hands away. "Uncle Teddy and Aunt Elena want to see you."

I went out into the hall, and my brother Ethan was there, his brown hair looking mussed, a worried expression on his round face. He came over. "How is he?"

"He's OK. Kind of drugged up, I think," I said, still thinking about what Grandpa had told me, what he'd made me promise.

A gorgeous woman, taller than me, with chocolate skin and her hair in braids, came over. Ethan turned and gestured. "Deb, this is Rebecca Akendele. She's in my econ class at school. She drove me here."

The woman held out her hand. "Call me Becky. Your brother has told me almost nothing about you." She had an

English accent; her voice was like music. She smiled, then she turned serious. "I know this is hard. You and Ethan love your grandfather."

I nodded a thanks.

Ethan headed for Grandpa's room. He looked back at Becky, but she shook her head, motioning for him to go on. I sat down and watched Uncle Teddy and Elena talking to Grandma. Olek, Voly, and the muscle were gone. I was sure the doctors and nurses were relieved.

Becky sat down beside me and took my hand, still a little sore where Grandpa had squeezed it. "Your grandfather is going to get better."

Ethan came out of Grandpa's room a few minutes later with a frown on his face. "I think he's OK. But he kept talking like you were in the room, Deb. Something…*vovchytsya*? What is that?"

I just shook my head.

પ્ર પ્ર પ્ર

Grandpa came home the next day. The hospital gave Grandpa a list of things to do to improve his health and "lower risk factors," including exercises to do and food no-no's—mostly salt and fat—which I knew wasn't going to change our Ukrainian-American diet. Salt and fat were its primary ingredients.

Grandpa, who had always been a rock, a safe place for me, looked old and frail. He went to the office every day, but we didn't go shooting on Sundays anymore.

A couple of weeks after Grandpa came home, I was in my room studying and listening to music on my phone on a Thursday night. Grandma had gone with our neighbor Mrs. Krasny to her church for some planning thing, and Grandpa was watching the news.

I heard the front doorbell and stuck my head out the door of my room to hear Grandpa say, "*Uviydit´, Teodor.*" "Come in, Teodor." I sat in my usual spot at the top of the stairs to listen.

"I will make some tea," I heard Grandpa say.

"No thank you, Viktor." I heard the scrape of dining room chairs on the floor.

"We have a problem. Let me show you," Uncle Teddy said. Paper rustling. "There are mistakes, errors. Invoices are here, but no goods. Bank deposit slips, but the money is not in the bank."

Boring. I tiptoed back to my room and put on my ear-buds. I was about to sit down when I heard Uncle Teddy's voice, very loud: "Someone is stealing from me!"

And then Grandpa, also loud: "I told you this months ago. You chose to ignore it."

Not boring. I went back to the stairs. Uncle Teddy was saying, "You were right, I was wrong. That is why I am here. You have always excellent records. Perhaps you can help clear this up."

"I will get my ledger." The scrape of a chair and Grandpa's footsteps. I heard his office door open. After a minute: "Let me see." Silence for two minutes.

More paper rustling. "Look at my records, at the bank statements, then at your records," Grandpa said. "See here, and here, and here. They do not agree. It must be someone in the *orhanizatsiyi*, Teo."

"No. It must be the Russians." Uncle Teddy spat out the word. "It was a mistake to join with them. They are trying to take over our business."

"That is something else I told you," Grandpa said, sighing.

"I thought so too. But Olek insisted. 'Better to join them than fight them,' he said."

"And they have access to your accounts, Teo?" Grandpa asked.

"No. It's not possible. But how do I know I won't find a Cayman Islands bank account in your name, old friend?"

Grandpa chuckled. "If my Nadiya were to hear you say that, she would stick a fork in your eye."

Uncle Teddy laughed. "I know. That is why I was sure to visit when she was not here. She has the temper, Viktor. You are always the calm one. The reasonable one. I will look into this further."

"You will not, I think, have far to look."

"What does that mean?"

"What I said." I heard Uncle Teddy's footsteps, then the front door opened and closed.

I went up to my room and got ready for bed.

CHAPTER 7

Friday night I was at Carol's house for a sleepover and to work on an American history project.

"Fifty-four forty or fight? Sounds like a commercial for chubby guys' clothes," I said.

Carol snorted Hansen's lemon-lime out her nose. "You are awful!"

"Yes, I am."

"We'd better actually get some writing done. This is due Monday," she said, running her fingers through her long blonde hair, of which I was unreasonably jealous. But I comforted myself with the fact that I was beating her time in cross-country by four minutes.

The front doorbell rang, and a minute later, Carol's mom, who kept insisting that I call her Ellen instead of Ms. Kendrick, brought in pizza, half-pepperoni (for me) and half mushroom and onion (for Carol). "Don't stay up too late," she said.

We ate pizza and watched something forgettable on Netflix. When we couldn't stall any longer, Carol sat down at her computer and started typing.

I got up off the floor and walked around her room,

looking at her posters of Rhianna and Chris Pratt and the photos of her and her boyfriend, Kyle, stuck on her big mirror. I had another brief thought about Rick and the other boys who had seemed interested in me but never stepped up. Maybe it was my mousy blonde hair or lack of boobs, I thought, looking in the mirror.

I laughed at myself. I came from a family of gangsters. Grigori Cogosin's run-in with Ethan and its aftermath had become a local legend, growing and changing into a beating in an alley by Ukrainian thugs. Stories of Grigori's sudden disappearance were possibly fueled by the fact that the Cogosins moved away soon after.

Carol and I finally gave up on American history and fell asleep with the TV on mute.

༺༺༺

Ellen came in and woke me up. It was still dark out. She was upset. "You have to…go home. Someone is coming to get you," she whispered.

"Why? What happened?"

She shook her head and went out the door. Carol rolled over in bed but didn't wake up as I got dressed and went into the living room.

I wanted to go wake up Carol, to tell her I was leaving, but Ellen stopped me. "No, no, don't bother. I'll tell her you had to go," she said, taking my arm with a sad smile. "Come sit here with me."

I pulled away from Ellen's hand and ran to the door, out and onto the porch, just as a black Lincoln pulled up to the curb and Voly got out. Behind me, Ellen opened the front door and brought out my backpack. Voly came up and, nodding to Ellen, took it with one hand. He took my arm with the other, and we walked to the car.

"Did Grandpa have another stroke? Is Grandma sick?"

"We are going to Teo's. We can talk there." Voly wouldn't look at me.

I wanted to know, and I didn't want to know. "Take me home first, Voly."

He shook his head. "We are going to Teo's." We got into the car and drove away. I looked over my shoulder. Ellen stood on the porch, watching.

"I need to get something at the house," I said. "I'll just run in and run out." Voly shook his head, his eyes on the road. A bubble, like stomach acid, rose up in me. Something had happened—something bad. "Take me home! Take me home!"

Voly just tightened his grip on the wheel, still not looking at me. "I am to bring you to Teo's."

We stopped at the signal on Avenue Y. I opened the car door and got out. Voly tried to grab me, but I was too fast. I ran across the parkway against the light, dodging the traffic. I ran down Ocean, under the Belt Parkway, crossed over to Neptune, down to Brighton 1st Street, over Ocean View. My breathing was fast and ragged. I couldn't get enough air. My chest had a knot that grew bigger as I ran, as I got closer to my home.

I ran around the corner onto Brighton 2nd Street— firetrucks and police cars with their lights flashing, an ambulance, a news van. I ran down the block, shoving through a crowd of neighbors and strangers on the sidewalks.

The whole front of my house was spewing smoke, which

drifted out the shattered front windows. Grandma's rose-bushes were trampled, squished flat. The front porch roof was scorched, its shingles smoking. Firemen coiled up hoses and shoveled through piles of stuff on the lawn. I ran up to the yellow plastic tape, and a big policeman got in front of me. "You can't—" he started, but I ducked under his outstretched arm and the tape and ran past him.

Afterward, our neighbor, Mrs. Krasny, told me I was screaming. I couldn't hear anything except the voice in my head: "No! No! No!"

Four firemen in red helmets and breathing masks came down the steps carrying two wheeled stretchers with black bags on them. On the front walkway, they pushed the wheels down and rolled them toward a tall black van.

Two giant arms grabbed me from behind. "Let go! Let go!" I fought and kicked, but the arms held me like steel bands. Then I was picked up and carried, still kicking, back to the sidewalk. A cop lifted the tape to let us pass. The big arms let go and put me down. I spun around and took a swing at whoever it was. It turned out to be Voly, who caught my fist like a whiffle ball pitch. Tears were running down his cheeks. He leaned over and hugged me so tightly it squeezed the breath out of me. "*Meni duzhe shkoda, meni duzhe shkoda,*" he said in a choked voice. I understood: "I'm so sorry, I'm so sorry."

I pulled away and sat on the wet sidewalk, my face in my hands. At some point, someone must have put me into Voly's car. I don't remember getting in or the ride to Uncle Teddy's big condo on Ocean. I sort of remember Aunt Elena sitting beside me on the couch in the living room, her arms around me. She said comforting things. I don't remember going to sleep in a big bedroom with red curtains and a TV on the wall. I don't remember crying. I don't think I did.

When I woke up, for a second, I thought I was in my room at home. Then I looked around, confused, at the strange pink wallpaper, the mirror with the gold frame, the jars of makeup on the white dresser, and the smell of perfume. I was wearing a long, lace-trimmed blue nightgown. Then I remembered. My grandparents were dead.

CHAPTER

The next two days at Uncle Teddy and Aunt Elena's condo were a sad movie, one I was in and was watching at the same time. I'd get up and go to the shiny kitchen, where there'd be eggs or cereal or something served by a thin-faced Somali woman in a white apron. She would look at me with round, sad eyes as if to speak, but she didn't.

Grandma and Grandpa had a lot of friends. They came to visit, and the Deborah in the movie smiled bravely at their sympathetic words, nodded at what seemed like the right times. Me, the other Deborah, watched, crouching and hidden in a misery closet.

Clean clothes appeared on the bed. Food appeared on a tray in the room. I think I must have eaten.

Monday, Ethan came to visit and sat with me a while. We didn't talk. Finally I asked, "Do you know...Do you know what happened?"

He began, "I don't...I don't..." He put his head in his hands and cried. I squeezed his shoulder, wanting to comfort him, but I couldn't comfort myself. I was jealous of his tears. I couldn't find any of my own.

"Grandma was getting absent-minded. Maybe she forgot to turn off the stove," I said.

Ethan didn't answer. After a minute, he stood up, wiping his eyes. "I'm sorry, Deb," he said. He waved his hand around the pink-wallpapered room. "For this. For not being there for you. I should have been a better brother." He walked to the door. "I'm going to the police, try to find out what happened. I'll let you know." He left.

Maybe Ethan could be a better brother. Or maybe I could be a better sister. It was too late to be a better granddaughter.

Later Olek saw me in the marble-floored hallway and gave me a hug.

"Do you know how the fire got started?" I asked, pulling away after a too-long time.

"Teo will tell you," Olek replied. He never called his father "papa" or "dad."

Aunt Elena only said, "Talk to Teodor," when I asked her. But Uncle Teddy wasn't around.

꒰ꜙ꒱ ꒰ꜙ꒱ ꒰ꜙ꒱

I mostly slept till noon. But that Tuesday, for some reason, I woke up early. I decided I'd go running. I put on my Millennium sweats, ankle socks, and tired Reeboks, took the elevator down, and jogged to the beach at Coney Island.

It was hard at first. After just a few days of no running, my legs were stiff, my breathing was ragged. The air was thick with moisture from the Sound, with the smell of exhaust from automobile tailpipes mixed with the odor of plants and dog poop, which I had to dodge on the sidewalk.

Left on Surf Avenue to Asser Levy Park. Into the park

to get away from the traffic and noise. I needed quiet on the outside to think. I didn't know why I was running. Maybe just to run. I didn't have to try to beat Brianna and fail; I didn't have to improve my interval time; I didn't have to make myself better. I just had to run.

Two laps around the park, and I started to get in tune again. I avoided traffic crossing Surf and headed for the boardwalk. My breathing got better, and the cramps that threatened went away.

I slowed my pace a little on the boardwalk. The Steeplechase Pier stretched into the Sound, a cool wind blowing into my face. I went down the pier to the end, where the morning fog was dissolving in the sun, Rockaway appearing like a ghost rising from the sea. A plane from Kennedy flew overhead, heading west. I thought about being a passenger on a plane, going somewhere else. But I was here. I was Deborah Sokolov, daughter of parents I couldn't remember, granddaughter of Viktor and Nadiya, whom I'd never forget.

I came back from my run and went upstairs. As I opened the door to the condo, I heard voices coming from the dining room.

"He killed them." Olek's voice.

Voly's voice: "So it seems. But the Russians have reasons, too. Teo, you said that Viktor had found some problems with the books. Constantin might want to hide things from us."

They were talking about my grandparents. Grandma didn't forget to turn the stove off. Grandpa didn't leave a cigar burning. Someone killed them. I felt my legs grow weak, not from running. I felt my heart beating faster, not from running.

"No! It wasn't the Russians!" Olek was angry, his voice

high-pitched. "The old man did it!" It was quiet for a moment. Then Olek spoke again. "Some people need killing."

"Olek!" Uncle Teddy's voice. "We do not do those things."

"We have friends in the prison to do it for us."

"Enough!" Uncle Teddy again, angry.

I walked into the dining room. Uncle Teddy, Olek, and Voly were sitting around the dining room table, the remains of a breakfast on it. "Why didn't you tell me that somebody murdered my grandparents?" I yelled. I felt my face turn red. My fists were clenched. Voly, Uncle Teddy, and Olek all stood up.

Olek said, "It would only make your pain worse, Deborah."

"How could it be any worse? Someone killed them. I want to know who!"

Uncle Teddy put his arm around me. "We can talk about this later, Deborah."

I shoved Uncle Teddy's arm away. I was a child to him, to all of them. "We can talk now. Who killed Grandma and Grandpa?"

Uncle Teddy looked over his shoulder. Voly stood up and came over. "I'll explain, Deborah," he said. Uncle Teddy nodded, clearly glad to have someone else deal with me.

We went into the overstuffed living room and sat down on the couch. Voly took my hand, and I pulled it away. "I'm not the little girl you used to push on the swing in the park. Just tell me what happened, who killed Viktor and Nadiya."

Voly told me what he knew: Anton Pavluk, an eighty-one-year-old Ukrainian man with cancer, had come to the house to kill my grandparents. He had turned himself in to the cops and confessed the next day. Voly looked away, biting his lip.

"Why?"

"I heard that he had a grudge against Viktor. Something from the old days in Ukraine," Voly replied.

"Grandma and Grandma left Ukraine thirty years ago!" I said, shaking my head in disbelief. "After all that time, now he…he…" I couldn't finish.

Voly shrugged. "Pavluk is sick, dying. Maybe he thought it was his last chance. He had little to lose." Voly took my hand again, and I let him. We sat for a while, not talking.

"Uncle Teddy came to visit Grandpa, the night before… before it happened. He said something about the Russians."

Voly shrugged. "I thought so too. But Olek asked our contacts in the police department. Pavluk was not connected with the Russians."

Pavluk had shot Viktor and Nadiya. So maybe they were dead when the fire started. They didn't have to feel the flames burning their flesh. I pushed away the picture in my head.

Voly stood up and took my hand to pull me to my feet. "Enough for now. You have to get ready for the services."

He meant my grandparents' funeral. I'd forgotten, but somewhere I'd remembered, and that was why I'd woken up early.

෧෧෧

Aunt Elena came in to help me get ready. Someone had bought me a black dress and shoes to wear. Aunt Elena fussed over my hair, which I hadn't brushed in a few days, and dabbed lipstick on my lips and eyeliner around my red eyes. I sat there like a store window dummy staring at the painted face in the gold-framed mirror. All made up for the movie.

"Perhaps this will be good for you, Deborah," Aunt Elena said. "Perhaps you will get closure."

"Closure? Like closing a door? I don't think so," I replied, as much to myself as to Aunt Elena. She shook her head sadly and went out.

The funeral service was to be held in Grandma's Ukrainian church on Nineteenth Street in Park Slope. Ethan drove me in the old Buick. I thought I'd hate riding in it, but the smell and feel was somehow comforting.

There were dozens of cars parked on both sides of the street. Women wearing black and men in gray suits with black armbands stood talking to one another on the sidewalk or walking up the steps to go inside. A black stretch limousine was parked at the front, a black hearse behind it. A traffic cop waved us into a parking spot and put a placard on the windshield.

Even from the outside, I could smell the incense. A memory came back: when Ethan and I used to come here with Grandma. I think I was supposed to cry. I dabbed my dry eyes with a handkerchief from a tiny black purse that Elena had given me.

We went up the stone steps and into the church. A woman with gray hair came over and hugged me. I didn't know her. She pulled a black headscarf from her purse and put it on me, tying it under my chin.

The church was filled with people, a lot of them old. Grandma and Grandpa had a lot of friends. Someone was playing an organ. Two shiny metal caskets covered with flowers were at the front, next to two wreaths of white flowers banded by red ribbons with Cyrillic writing. The gray-bearded priest, wearing a black robe and a black pointy hat, stood on the dais behind them. Ethan, in a gray jacket with a black armband, took my arm, and we walked down the aisle. Heads turned, eyes stared. We sat in the front pew with Elena, Uncle Teddy, and Olek, who reached over and patted my hand.

Suddenly I felt like I was in a coffin, squeezing me tighter and tighter. I couldn't breathe. The gray stone columns on either side were pressing in, leaning over to crush me.

I got up and ran down the aisle, heading outside. I bumped into an old lady in black, almost knocking her over. I heard voices. Then Ethan called, "Deb!" Heads turned to look at me as I ran.

Outside, I took a breath, my hands on my knees. I took off the scarf and the too-tight shoes. I tossed them and the tiny purse onto the steps as I ran down to the sidewalk. I ran. I ran and ran. Down Nineteenth Street to McDonald, down past the Green-Wood Cemetery, where I ran on the grass. I crossed Fort Hamilton and cars honked at me, but I didn't care. I kept running. Along McDonald Avenue, past a school, across Caton Avenue and more honking, a squeal of brakes, and someone yelling something.

Then under the El, trucks jamming the road on either side, but I could dodge and zig and zag between giant bumpers. Even slowing down, I felt the wind on my face, my heart pumping, my blood coursing through me.

I ran some more, ignoring the pain, "pushing through it," as Coach Robbins would say. I ran, my breathing regular and fast, my legs loosening, feeling the wind blow through my hair.

Running. Running. I crossed Ocean still breathing

easily. Then I stepped on something sharp. I hopped over to the curb and sat down. I put my left foot on my knee and pulled out a piece of glass.

A big man in a hard hat stopped nearby. "Are you OK?"

I nodded. He went over to a ConEd van parked next to an open manhole and spoke to a younger guy with long hair, also in a hard hat. They looked over at me. I got up and limped away, leaving a bloody trail.

రావాల

I arrived at my home. Broken yellow tape hung on the stair railing. There was plywood over the front windows and door, and a pile of furniture and burned stuff on the lawn. I limped up the cracked cement walkway to the back porch, unlocked the door with the key that was always under the mat, and went into the kitchen.

It smelled like smoke. The fire had burned mostly in the front of the house—the living room and Grandpa's office. I thought I'd feel bad and guilty about running away from my grandparents' funeral. I didn't feel anything at all. Maybe that would come later. Or not. I went upstairs to my room. It smelled like smoke. I fell face-down on my bed, drifting in a dark sea.

I woke up hearing Ethan's voice. "Deb? Are you here?"

Fragments of a dream slid out of my mind. Grandpa and Grandma were in it. It was early evening. I sat up and called out, my voice like a frog's, "In my room."

Ethan came upstairs. The streetlight outside lit up his worried face. He was still in his gray jacket and armband. He sat down beside me on the bed.

He was my big brother. He was always on my case: "Do this. Don't do that." He was going to yell at me for bailing on the funeral. He said nothing, just put his arm around me. After a minute, he said, "It was a nice service."

"I'm sorry." That was mostly true.

"There was a gathering afterward at Uncle Teddy's. A lot of people, friends of Viktor and Nadiya. A lot of people who loved them." Ethan leaned over, lifted my leg, and looked at my bloody foot. "That's gotta hurt." I shrugged.

He got up and went into the bathroom, returning with gauze, tape, a towel, a washcloth, and a basin. He knelt on the floor in front of me and washed my feet, pouring alcohol over the cuts. It hurt, but I didn't yell, I just kind of squinched up my face and bit my lip. He taped on the gauze.

"The water's turned back on. Go wash your face and get some other clothes." Ethan got up and went downstairs.

I washed up, then put on jeans and a sweatshirt. They didn't smell of smoke. I tried my Adidas, but they hurt my foot. I got my sandals from under the bed and slipped them on.

Ethan stood looking out the window in the empty and dark living room. He came over and took my arm. "Come on."

"I can't go back there," I said, meaning Uncle Teddy's condo. "Not now. Not yet."

"We're not going there."

☙☙☙

Ethan parked on Cooper Avenue in front of a closed florist's across the street from the Holy Trinity Cemetery that was bordered by a low concrete block wall. The gate was locked.

He boosted me up to the top of the wall, saying, "Give me a hand. I'll catch you on the other side."

"Oh yeah. My foot." I reached down to pull him up.

We walked, me limping, about a half-mile in. A grove of trees encircled two freshly dug gravesites covered with a tarp. I plucked some flowers from a nearby grave, silently apologizing to Irena Oliynyk, Beloved Wife, Mother and Sister, December 12, 1929–August 17, 2016, and went over to stand next to Ethan.

"Our parents are over there," Ethan said, pointing to a pair of headstones. I'd not been here since I was little, but I remembered. *Peter & Susan Sokolov, died September 20, 2004.*

I lifted the green plastic sheet from our grandparents' graves and placed the stolen flowers on each one. We stood there, not saying anything. Ethan put his arm around me, and I leaned into him. I remembered what Grandma used to say when she tucked me in at night: "*Na dobranich.*" "Sleep well."

CHAPTER 9

Three days later, I was running out of clothes at Uncle Teddy's. Aunt Elena said she'd send someone over to get my things. I didn't want strangers messing with my stuff, so I decided I'd go. Voly drove me in one of the *orhanizat-siyi´s* black SUVs. The workmen weren't there, but things were getting done. The burned stuff was gone, the porch roof had new shingles, the windows had new glass, and the house was freshly painted in the same white with green trim as before. But a piece of plywood covered the front doorway. A dented green storage container sat on the driveway behind the old Buick.

Voly asked, "Do you need help?" I shook my head, got out, and went up the walkway. Our neighbor, Mrs. Krasny, was outside watering her flowers. She and Grandma used to trade insider secrets for the best roses. She came to the fence and beckoned to me. I leaned over as she hugged me. "I feel for you. I know you loved Viktor and Nadiya. And they loved you and Ethan like their own children. "

I nodded and smiled. "Thank you."

"You know, it was my husband who reported the fire," Mrs. Krasny said, walking over to our yard. She said that

Yakov had gotten up to go to the bathroom, as he did several times a night, and he looked out the window when he heard a car driving off very fast.

"Yakov is an auto mechanic, you know," Mrs. Krasny said. An image came to mind: a tall, stringy-brown-haired man sitting on the Krasnys' porch in blue coveralls, drinking a beer and waving at me. "He did not see the car, but he could tell by the sound of the engine that it was very powerful."

She said her husband saw the flames inside the house and yelled at her to call 911. He ran outside, grabbed the garden hose—"This very one," she said, waving the green coiled hose in her hand. "He tried to put out the fire, but it was not long enough to reach."

"Tell Mr. Krasny thank you," I said. But Grandma and Grandpa were still dead.

I went inside, where it smelled of fresh paint, not smoke. The living room and office were still empty, the furniture in the container outside, I guessed. Painters' tarps, buckets, and pans were everywhere.

Voly told me his brother-in-law did all the work. Everything would be done by the end of the week, "and it will be like new." Voly wanted to make me feel better. I wanted to feel better, to feel something, to fill the hole where my feelings should be.

I took a suitcase from the closet upstairs and put my clothes in it. I stuffed my laptop and schoolbooks into my backpack. I looked around my room. It looked like somebody else's room, somebody younger.

I opened a drawer of my dresser, and there was an old cigar box of Grandpa's. The torn label read Arturo Fuente. A memory of Grandpa came back, sitting outside in the back yard smoking his cigar because Grandma wouldn't let him smoke in the house. I flipped open the lid and saw the seashells I'd collected when Grandma and Grandpa, Ethan, and I went to Coney Island in the summer. Sand dollars, oysters, mussels, and one, called a whelk—fat, white, with reddish-brown stripes and seven pointy things on the end. Some other Deb would cry.

On the way back to Uncle Teddy's, I asked Voly, "Anton Pavluk. What do you know about him?"

Voly glanced over then back at the road. "He has liver cancer. He owned a carpet store that went out of business, and he was living on Social Security. His wife is dead. A son, married, lives in Queens. Pavluk lived in Brooklyn, Sheepshead Bay, for twenty-some years."

"He's practically a neighbor for that long, and just now decides to...to..." I couldn't finish.

"He turned himself into the police. They found the gun in his apartment. It...it matched." Voly couldn't say it. The bullets in my grandparents came from his gun. I felt tears again and pushed them away.

Voly pulled over to the curb and turned to me. "There's a sentencing hearing tomorrow. But you don't want to go."

My baby-sitter and buddy, telling me what I want. "Yeah, I do."

❧❧❧

The Kings County Criminal courtroom was almost empty except for two old men sitting in the back. They probably came every day to watch the real reality show. Ethan, Uncle Teddy, Aunt Elena, and I entered as a white-haired and bearded judge shuffled through papers and through a procession of gloomy guys getting sentenced to prison. No jury. No lawyers arguing. No drama.

On the other side of the wooden railing, a chubby lady with her brown hair in a ponytail stood up. "Case docket 347-dash-0045, Anton Pavluk." A man with slicked-back hair in a shiny blue suit stepped forward. "Robert Garza for Mr. Pavluk, your honor." A bailiff opened a side door in the windowless wood-paneled courtroom and another bailiff entered, holding a skinny old man in an orange DOC jumpsuit, with limp gray hair and skin the color of a squash. He staggered and stumbled, and the bailiff had to hold him up. This was the killer of my grandparents. He put a shaking hand down on the table as he slumped into a wooden chair next to the lawyer.

A serious-looking blonde woman sitting at another table stood up. "Ann O'Brian for the District Attorney's office, your honor. Mr. Garza has entered a plea of guilty for his client, Mr. Pavluk, on the two counts of murder in the second degree, and our office has accepted it." It was just like a TV show, except my grandparents were dead. Garza took Pavluk's arm and helped him to his feet.

"Do you understand the charges against you?" the judge asked. Pavluk nodded. "You have to answer, Mr. Pavluk."

"I understand," he said in a strained voice.

"Do you have anything to say to before I pass sentence?"

Pavluk shook his head, and Garza nudged him. "No."

The judge looked down at some papers then looked at Pavluk. "Anton Pavluk, for the crime of two counts of murder in the second degree, I hereby sentence you to ten years in a minimum-security prison. Because of your age and medical condition, the District Attorney has agreed to Mr. Garza's request for a lesser sentence than I might otherwise have been inclined to approve."

The judge looked at us where we were sitting in the front row. "The family of the victims is here. If any of you have something to say to Mr. Pavluk, now is the time." Ethan glanced over at Aunt Elena, Uncle Teddy, and Olek, who exchanged looks and shook their heads. This is the scene in TV shows where the victims either condemn or forgive. Not me. I stood up. Ethan tugged at my sleeve.

I took a breath and stood up, facing Pavluk. "I have something." Pavluk kept looking down at the floor. "I'm the granddaughter of Viktor and Nadiya Sokolov, the people you killed." He looked up at me then back at the floor.

"Why did you murder them?" I asked, trying to picture this shaky old guy as a killer. Grandpa could have taken him down with a single right hook. Grandma could have knocked him over with her beloved Uzbek cast-iron frying pan.

Pavluk looked at me then motioned to the guard to take him away. As they went out, I yelled, "Why did you kill them? Why?"

The judge spoke up. "Please, Ms. Sokolov. I know this is difficult, but the law has run its course."

I walked fast out of the courtroom. In the echoing hallway I found a wooden bench to sit on. I'd come here thinking maybe it would be over, or start to be over. It wasn't. Small, sharp-edged things, like broken glass or pieces of metal, took up residence in my head. Maybe it was brain cancer or slivers of broken glass from the old front door of the house on East Second Street, Brighton Beach. A word from History Channel documentaries: shrapnel, the metal fragments from an exploded bomb or hand grenade that wound and kill those outside the blast.

Uncle Teddy, Aunt Elena, and Ethan came out of the courtroom. Ethan sat beside me.

"There, there, dear," Aunt Elena said, handing me a handkerchief from her purse. "Don't cry." I wasn't crying.

Ethan stood up and took my arm. "It's time to go home, Deb." I started down the hall with Ethan holding my hand. Uncle Teddy and Aunt Elena followed. Pavluk's lawyer came out of the courtroom behind us, and I pulled away from Ethan and ran back down the hall. The lawyer got into an elevator, and the door closed. I sprinted to the end of the hall and ran down the stairs.

The elevator doors opened as I arrived on the ground floor. Pavluk's lawyer stepped out, reacting with wide eyes as I came up to him. "Uh…Ms. Sokolov? Can I help you?"

"I don't know," I replied. "It's just…I don't understand. I'm having a hard time seeing that man…as the killer of my grandparents." I smiled a small, sad smile, wiping away tears that weren't there. "Anything you could tell me might help."

The lawyer took my hand. "My name's Garza. There's a coffee shop down the hall." He walked off, and I knew I had his sympathy.

Garza brought over two coffees, and we sat at the small plastic table. Cops, crooks, serious men and women in suits walked by. "I know this must be hard for you. I understand your grandparents raised you."

I nodded. "If you could tell me more, maybe I could kind of…at least start to accept it."

"Closure," Garza said with a knowing nod. Not happening. I didn't say anything. He reached down to his briefcase and pulled out a folder. "I have copies of Mr. Pavluk's state-ment and the District Attorney's report. If that would help."

"Maybe. But I was wondering… I didn't see anyone from his family at the hearing. Who hired you?"

Garza flipped through some pages. "A while ago, Mr. Pavluk's son, Mikhail, asked me to handle his father's court appearances. The next day, a cashier's check to cover costs was messengered to our office," he replied.

"Do you really think he did it?" I asked.

Garza looked out the window, then back at me. "It's not my job to determine if my client is guilty or innocent, Deborah. It's my job to represent him."

He looked at his phone. "I have a meeting." He handed me the pages with his business card clipped on them. "You can keep these copies. My cell phone number is on the card. I hope this will help you move on with your life."

"Closure," I said with a nod and a little smile. Garza stood up, patted me sympathetically on my shoulder, and left. I took a sip of coffee and spit it back in the cup.

My phone beeped. It was Ethan. "Where are you?" I text-ed Ethan that I'd take the train. I'd put on a little show for him, like the one I'd been putting on for Aunt Elena, Uncle Teddy, Garza, even my brother. I was a brave but sad little girl, just holding it together. On the inside, the other me was wounded by shrapnel, or sharp pieces of glass from the windows in the burned house on Brighton 2nd Street.

❧❧❧

On the F train going home, I went through the DA's report. At 11:44 p.m., 911 logged a call from Mrs. Krasny reporting a fire. NYFD Engine companies 245 and 246 arrived at 11:50 p.m. and put out the fire in about fifteen minutes. The police were called when my grandparents' bodies were found. Arson investigators determined that the fire started around 11:30 p.m. in the living room using an accelerant, probably gasoline. The medical examiner reported that Nadiya and Viktor Sokolov had been both found in the living room. They'd both been shot. I couldn't read the details: the bullets fired, the entry and exit wounds, the damage to bone and tissue. The medical examiner determined that they were already deceased when the fire started.

At 2:45 a.m., Anton Pavluk showed up at the 60th Precinct and confessed to the crime. Uniformed officers went to his apartment and found the weapon, a Russian Tokarev, under Pavluk's mattress. Ballistics proved the bullets came from that gun. Pavluk's fingerprints were on it.

Pavluk's confession was one paragraph, and I had to force myself to read it. He was getting revenge for Grandpa killing his brother forty years ago in Ukraine. He killed Grandma when she came at him with a kitchen knife—a knife that was still in her hand when the firemen found her body. That was it. I put the folder in my backpack.

I ate dinner by myself in the room with pink wallpaper and red curtains. On my way out of the condo, Elena caught me and fussed over me, worried about my being on my own. But I couldn't look at myself in that gold-framed mirror anymore, couldn't stay in the room that smelled of Coco Mademoiselle, couldn't watch any more History Channel on the giant TV in the wood-paneled den that stank of cigarettes. Uncle Teddy and Olek went out to do whatever they did at their warehouse, and Aunt Elena went shopping. I shoved my clothes into my backpack and I left.

❧❧❧

The repairs to the house on Second Street were done. The orange dumpster was gone, and the tiny lawn was getting green. Someone had staked the rosebushes, which were just showing little red buds. The new front door had glass panes like the old one, but plain, not with the old, beveled glass squares that distorted the view when I'd looked through them. One old thing was Grandpa's Buick in the driveway. The bumper that Grandma had dented when she drove to the hospital had been replaced.

An invoice from All-American Home on the front hall table showed that they'd delivered new furniture made in China. The living room and Grandpa's office were pretty much new.

There was a new green couch where the saggy maroon couch used to be, a slick leather chair in place of the raggedy old one where Grandpa sat and read *Svoboda* (Liberty), the Ukrainian newspaper that came in the mail on Wednesdays. Grandma's straight-backed rocking chair was gone too, where she sometimes read our old Ukrainian Bible or crocheted booties for some cousin's or niece's new baby. Grandma's favorite rose-patterned wallpaper had been replaced with an off-white paint.

In the dining room, they'd been able to save our table, chairs, and glass-fronted sideboard, a "hootch" Grandma called it, meaning hutch. Her old rose-trimmed plates and cups, only for special occasions, were still inside it.

The kitchen cabinets, freshly painted, were full of food: cans of chicken soup, tuna (which only me and Ethan ever ate), packages of cold cereal and oatmeal. Another cabinet held new plates, cups, and dishes where Grandma used to store her "for everyday" tableware. A wire container on the new granite-looking countertop held bananas and apples. Under the counter next to the sink, a steel-fronted dishwasher took the place of a few drawers. A shiny steel refrigerator had milk, eggs, Ukrainian cheeses, and yogurt. Boxes of frozen dinners filled the freezer. Voly, knowing my suboptimal cooking skills, probably chose them. I thought I might be hungry, but I couldn't tell.

Grandpa's office still had his old chair, but a new desk occupied the floor, and a new empty bookcase was against the wall. A handwritten note on the desk mentioned a box in the garage containing the stuff the workers had been able to salvage. I wondered if the gray metal box with the Nagant had been saved. Somehow, they'd managed to rescue the old pendulum clock, still hanging on the wall, still ticking away. Someone, probably Voly again, had been coming in to wind it.

I sat in Grandpa's office chair and leaned back, hearing the squeaky springs. I put my face in the cushion. No smell from the fire, but a faint odor of Grandpa's cigars and a faint voice in my head: Grandpa's.

Have you done your homework, Deborah?

I went upstairs. My room was the same. The Almaz Ayana poster on the wall, a bookshelf with mostly second-place trophies from my cross-country meets, a fluffy pale-pink comforter on my bed. Somebody had stacked my laptop, three-ring binder, and textbooks on my desk, and I remembered: The day after tomorrow I was supposed to go back to Brooklyn Millennium High School.

My phone rang. It was Ethan calling, but I didn't feel like talking. I fell onto my bed and immediately went to sleep.

I'm running beside a fence, a wooden fence. My breathing is fast and regular. My leg muscles are taut and strong. I could run like this forever. The sun is bright, but I'm not even a little bit hot.

Then I see a head bobbing up and down on the other side of the fence, keeping pace with me. There's someone on the other side, but I can't see who it is. Suddenly my breath gets short and labored, my legs start to cramp. The head on the other side passes me by, running, running. I have to find out who it is, find out who's beating me. I am angry. I can barely move. My feet feel like someone's grabbing them, holding me back. Then suddenly the fence ends. I fall on my knees, turning my head to see the person on the other side of the fence. And then I wake up.

CHAPTER

As I walked down the scuffed vinyl hallway heading to homeroom, I was two people again. The outside me belonged to a girl who could put one foot in front of the other; who could nod at friends when they made caring noises; who could smile at the principal, Mr. Zapata, when he came out of his office and took my hand in both of his, smiling sympathetically. I was two Debs again: one, a puppet on strings pulled by everyone's expectations, having the feelings and attitudes that were expected of her. The other Deb was somewhere else, angry, running alongside a fence with someone behind it that she couldn't see.

People I'd been friends with since fourth grade made sure to step aside and pretend to be talking to someone else when I walked down the hall. Teachers who usually called on me avoided even looking in my direction. Who knew that you became infectious when your grandparents got murdered? In third period AP math, I sat in the back of the room and made doodles in my notebook.

Carol came up to me in the hall after class and gave me a hug. "I'm sorry. I don't know what to say," she said.

"Nobody does," I said. She took my arm and led me to

the lunch area. Carol shared her yogurt with me since I'd forgotten to bring anything. The awkwardness was getting weird. I got up. "I gotta go," I said.

Coach Robbins found me on a bench in the yard and asked me if I wanted to come back to the cross-country team. I said no. She was disappointed.

"Running might be a good thing for you to do now," she said.

"I'll think about it," I replied. I'd felt good for about an hour while running away from my grandparents' funeral. But it didn't last.

Alexandra, a friend from middle school who'd turned into a mean girl, came over and sat next to me. "I lost my grandparents too," she said, not mean. "I know how you're feeling." I didn't think so. Alexandra's grandparents probably died peacefully of old age surrounded by family, not by being murdered.

I nodded. "Thanks." I knew she was trying to be kind, but I'd built a wall, or a scab, between me and others' pity. Maybe it was a Ukrainian thing.

Millennium High School was suddenly a foreign country where I knew nobody and didn't speak the language. I left when lunch period ended.

☙☙☙

That afternoon, Aunt Elena came over, letting herself in. She carried a foil-covered dish that she took into the kitchen and put in the oven. Then she took my arm and led me into the living room. We sat on the couch. "The school called," she said.

"I just couldn't do it, *Titon'ka* Elena. I just couldn't," I said.

Elena patted my back. "I know, I know. Maybe you would be better if you came back to stay with us for a few more days." She looked around the room. "Too many bad memories here."

"Good memories too. Good memories," I said, arguing with myself as much as with her. "If I can't be here, it's like I'm leaving even those behind." After another half-hour of sympathy, Aunt Elena took the dish out of the oven and left me alone in the house. I put the dish in the fridge.

 •••

On Wednesday afternoon, Ethan called. "Got some news. But how are you doing? How's school?"

"I'm fine," I said. "I ran a personal best two hundred meters today."

A silence. Then, "Oh? Maybe around the block? You ditched school at lunch Monday."

I'm an amateur liar. Getting nailed pissed me off. "Yeah! Try hanging out with people who pretend you're not there, who walk the other way when they see you coming!"

"So now you give a crap what other people think?"

"I…just couldn't do it, Ethan. I need more time," I said. Lame, but the best I could do.

"Fine. Just don't try to bullshit me." I heard his sigh. "But let me tell you something that might make you feel better."

Ethan had been to see the family's lawyer and learned that that the house was paid off, Grandma and Grandpa had life insurance worth about half a million dollars, and there was a trust fund for our education of two hundred thousand bucks.

"That's great," I said. I didn't feel better, but I wanted to get Ethan off my case.

"I almost believe you," he said. I had to get better at lying to my brother. "If you need more time, we can arrange a leave of absence or something." He sighed again. "Sometimes I want to go sit in a quiet room and not see anybody. But it helps me to keep doing stuff. My classes, the computer lab."

"So you just forget what happened?"

"I'll never forget what happened, Deb. Never."

∾∾∾

On Thursday, I got up around noon. In the mail was a fat envelope containing a checkbook and a credit card, both with my name on them, along with a note from Ethan: *Don't go nuts. I'm monitoring the accounts every day.* I thought about going on a shopping spree but couldn't think of anything I wanted. I went back to bed.

I didn't wake up again until Friday, when I heard a car pull up outside, the picture of a wooden fence fading like the end of a movie. I looked out my window to see Ethan's friend Becky get out of a silver BMW. I put on my ratty, lime-green bathrobe and went downstairs.

Becky came in with a green tote bag. "Kitchen?" she asked. I pointed. I followed her. She took a thermos and some plastic containers from the bag. She opened the refrigerator and looked surprised. "Lots of food. Are you eating?"

I shrugged. "Sometimes."

Becky stared at me and wrinkled her nose. "Go shower," she said, and I obeyed.

When I came back downstairs all clean and spiffy, the dining room table was set with a pitcher of something red, plates with eggs and toast, and two mugs of coffee. "Sit," Becky said, and again I obeyed. Despite my tendency to do the opposite of what people want, this was kind of fun.

Becky poured from the pitcher into my glass, and I took a sip. "Wow. I was expecting fruit punch." It was sweet, with a little bite.

"It's called zobo," Becky said. "Made from the hibiscus plant. I put in a little chili."

I drank it down. "This is good." I looked over at her as she buttered her toast. "I'm guessing you're not here to make me breakfast. Did Ethan send you?"

Becky shook her head. "Ethan doesn't send me any- where." She pointed with the butter knife to my plate. "Eat first. Then we'll talk."

After breakfast, Becky carried the plates into the kitchen and stacked them on the pile in the sink. She pointed to the brand-new dishwasher under the counter. "Do you use this?" I started to say something, but she waved her hand. "Never mind. Help me load." Again, I obeyed.

"So, what do you want to do now?" Becky asked as we sat down on the new couch in the living room.

"I don't know. Maybe watch a movie," I replied, knowing that's not what she meant.

Becky stood up, folded her arms, and stared at me. "So you're just going to sit on your skinny ass in your stinky bathrobe and feel sorry for yourself?" She shook her head. "I didn't take you for a loser. I guess I was wrong."

I jumped up to face her. "You don't get it! You don't know." I grabbed her arm and pulled her to the hallway. "Get out! Leave me alone!" I opened the door.

Becky snorted. "No wonder Ethan was so upset. He thought you were better than this. So did I. Pathetic."

I raised my hand to hit her, to slap her, to make her go away, but she grabbed my wrist.

"I have to get my things." She pushed past me and headed for the kitchen.

I flopped back down on the couch and wrapped my arms around my knees. "Don't forget your zombie or whatever you call it," I yelled.

Becky came back with her tote bag. She started for the door then put down her bag and came back to sit next to me on the couch. I turned away. "The door is over there," I said, waving my hand.

Becky took out her phone, tapped it a few times, then showed me a photo of a smiling group: a woman dressed in a bright green-and-black dashiki; a tall, bearded man in a suit wearing a white knit cap; two girls, one older, one younger, both with big eyes staring shyly at the camera.

"Your family. Good for you."

"My mother was a schoolteacher, my father was a civil servant working in agriculture. I was away at school in England when Boko Haram came to our town. They…they murdered them. Even my little sister, because she was in school, and school is forbidden to girls." Becky looked at me, tears running down her cheeks. "For a long time, I was sad and hollow inside, you know?" I knew exactly. "I dropped out of school. For months, I sat in my room staring at the wall. I wanted to die." Becky pulled her bracelets up her arm to show me a scar on her left wrist. "I didn't do a very good job. My roommate found me and took me to A and E—the emergency ward."

All of a sudden, some drain plug in my body got yanked out. Everything—all the armor I'd carefully made, the hollows that had pushed feelings aside, every moment, every thought—just flushed out of me. Behind them, the sadness came flooding through me. It had been stored up in the days I might have cried but didn't. The glass shards in my head fractured again, and there was pain, but not for me. Not just for me. I leaned over and hugged Becky, and she hugged me back. My tears soaked the shoulder of her yellow blouse, her tears soaked the shoulder of my Millennium sweatshirt.

Later we washed our streaked faces in the front bathroom. We looked at ourselves in the mirror and laughed. "I'm sorry," I said. "I was being a jerk."

"I did the same thing," Becky said. "I pushed away people who tried to be there for me." I handed her a towel, and she wiped her face. "I have something for you," she said and went into the living room.

Becky reached into her tote bag and took out a matted, unframed picture carefully wrapped in clear plastic. She handed it to me. "I made this for you."

It was a pastel drawing: gray skies, a snowy landscape, mountains and trees, and standing there looking out, a gray wolf darker against the sky, with white and silver down its chest. I stared at it, disbelieving. I remembered Grandpa taking my hand and squeezing so tightly it hurt: *Vovchytsya.* I looked up: "How did you…Why?" I couldn't finish.

Becky took the picture and leaned it against a table lamp. "At the hospital, Ethan told me your grandfather seemed agitated, upset. He kept telling Ethan to watch out for you, saying things in Ukrainian. He kept repeating one word: *Vovchytsya.* I googled it. She-wolf."

I took the picture and held it to my chest. "I love it. Thank you."

"You're welcome," Becky said. Then she turned serious. "Tell me: do you believe this man who confessed killed your grandparents?"

I knew the answer, even though I'd never asked myself the question: "No," I said.

I retrieved the police report from my backpack and gave it to Becky. I told her about the day I saw Pavluk in court, about what Mrs. Krasny told me about the car, and mostly my gut feeling. "He was old and weak." I held up my hands, shaking them. "He was like this. How did he hold a gun? And somebody paid for his lawyer."

"It's all very neat and tidy. Same-day delivery, like Fe-dEx," Becky said, scanning the pages. She put them down and took my shoulders in her hands, looking at me. "Lots of unanswered questions. Do you want answers or not?"

"Yeah. No. Partly I want to, you know, move on, let it go." I looked out my front window, fighting tears. "Everyone keeps telling me 'Get closure,'" I almost shouted. "You know what closure is? It's a scab over a wound that won't heal."

Becky nodded, looking out the window. "I know."

I wiped my eyes. Something boiled up in me, burning like acid. The fingernails of my left hand dug into my palm. My right hand felt the metal and wood grip of the Nagant, the raised diamond patterns pressing into my skin. I almost looked down to see if they were there.

Splintering fragments drove a dark and shapeless

thought into my head. I pushed it away. Maybe it was justice, or maybe not. Whatever it was, it wasn't "letting go."

"You said your neighbor heard a car driving away just before he saw the fire. But there's nothing here about that."

I shook my head. "Pavluk confessed. I guess the police didn't bother."

Becky stood up. "If there was a car, perhaps some security camera down on the avenue got a picture of it."

"Yeah. Or maybe it was just a car. Or maybe there's no cameras anywhere." I sounded like second-place Deb.

She took my hand and pulled me to my feet. "Let's go for a walk."

కు కు కు

A lot of businesses on the avenue had video surveillance. Maybe one of those cameras was working on that Thursday night, almost three weeks ago, maybe it was pointed in the right direction, maybe it saw the car driven by my grandparents' killer coming out of Second Street. This was me talking myself out of it as Becky and I walked down my street, looking up at the buildings for cameras. On our one-way street, the car would be heading south, turning left or right on Brighton Beach Avenue, or continuing on toward the channel.

Grandpa and Grandma had lived in the neighborhood since before I was born, so most of the local business owners knew us. Kamal at ABC Produce on the corner showed us his fancy surveillance setup with one camera pointing right up Second Street. But no video storage; the recordings were erased every morning. Cameras on the shoe store and the clothing store weren't pointing in the right direction.

"We should try the other side of the street," Becky said.

"The El blocks the view," I said.

"Perhaps, perhaps not," Becky replied. "It depends on where the camera is."

We walked crossed the avenue, dodging rush hour traffic. Mr. Gorodsky's *apteka*, or pharmacy, was three doors down from the corner. On the wall was a camera tucked in next to the jewelry store.

"We only have it on at night, when we're closed," Mr. Gorodsky, round, bald, and smiling, told us. I had to endure more condolences.

Mrs. Gorodsky, also round, but not bald, came out and gave me a hug. "It was a very nice funeral," she said, and again I felt guilty for running away.

We followed Mrs. Gorodsky into the rear of the pharmacy, where she sat at a monitor with a split screen view: one camera showing the rear of the building, the other pointed at the street, under the El. We could see the ABC Produce awning and about halfway up the east side of Second Street. "Ruffians tried to break in few months ago, so I persuaded Anatoly to join the twenty-first century," she said. "Drug addicts! Feh!" she spat, clicking her mouse as she looked for the video files.

Becky said, "I can do it—"

Mrs. Gorodsky snorted a laugh. "Children! You think no one older than fifty knows anything about computers." I think Becky blushed. "What's the date, Deborah?"

"May fourteenth," I replied. "After eleven thirty," I added, remembering what the arson investigators had determined. Mrs. Gorodsky typed and clicked furiously, and the monitor zipped through scenes, fast-reversing, cars and pedestrians going backward, going back in time, back to that night. There it was, in the left corner of the screen: 05-14.

There was lots of traffic on Brighton Beach Avenue, but no cars coming down Second Street. "Forward a little more," I said, afraid of what I might see. There, at 11:40 p.m., May 14, an orange glow lit up the street at the limit of the camera's view, reflecting off the parked cars and the windows of the houses across the street. Mrs. Gorodsky looked over her shoulder at me and blanked the screen. "I'm sorry. I didn't realize what…what you wanted. Maybe you shouldn't be seeing this?"

I shook my head. "It's all right."

Becky gave me a quick hug. She turned to Mrs. Gorodsky. "Could we have a copy? Just that date?"

"Of course, dear," Mrs. Gorodsky said.

Becky dug into her purse. "I have a USB thingy here somewhere…"

Mrs. Gorodsky was quicker. She pulled a thumb drive from a drawer and put it in a slot on the monitor. Another minute, and she removed the drive and handed it to Becky, then she got up and kissed me on both cheeks.

"Need a little help, dear," Mr. Gorodsky called from the front.

"Coming, dear," Mrs. Gorodsky replied. She got up from her chair, and we followed her back into the pharmacy. Mr. Gorodsky, looking frazzled, was facing a line of customers at the counter. He waved as we went out.

I kicked an empty plastic water bottle across the avenue, which smacked into the rusty metal pillar of the El. "What a waste of time," I said as we crossed the street. "There's nothing."

Becky waved her hand, pushing away my 'tude. "Be patient. We just had two minutes. You should take another look at the footage. What if it was a motorcycle? It might have been hidden behind a car passing by. What if whoever it was, was on foot?"

"But Mr. Krasny said he heard a car—"

Becky stepped in front of me, grabbing my arms. A train rumbled and squealed by overhead. Traffic rushed by us on both sides. We were an island in the middle of a fast-flowing current, a river that could sweep us away.

The traffic light changed, and we crossed the street. I started to walk home, but Becky stopped me. "You have a decision to make."

I looked down at the cracked sidewalk, over Becky's shoulder to the graffiti on the brick wall of ABC Produce. Anywhere but at her dark eyes.

The two Deborahs were at war. Maybe in a month—or months—from now, I could get back to something like a life. The wounds wouldn't heal, but scab over. The shrapnel would stop hurting.

ॐॐॐ

We went up the walk to my front door. Becky took my hand. "Let's sit for a moment." We sat on the steps. Becky tucked her finger under my chin and turned my head to face her. "What do you know?"

"Nothing, except somebody, not Pavluk, killed my grandparents." I thought for a second. "Uh, and Mr. Krasny saw the fire and heard a car drive down the street."

"Okay. So if it wasn't whatshisname, then who? And why?"

I told Becky about Uncle Teddy's visit. The night before it happened. She nodded. "So maybe something to do with the gangster business."

I shrugged. "Maybe. Not Uncle Teddy, though."

Becky stood up. "Think about it some more. We'll talk." She retrieved her bag from the house, got in her shiny Beemer and drove off.

❧ ❧ ❧

I was in the bathroom on Saturday morning when my phone rang. It was a video call from a smiling Becky. "Hey, sister. I've got some news. How are you doing?"

I turned on my camera to show Becky. "Ushing ay eeth."

"Call me back when you've finished your ablutions."

I spit the toothpaste into the sink. "Ablutions. Is that a Princeton word?"

"Yes. But if you're nice, we of the High Council will let you use it. Can you come over?"

"It's seven in the morning. What news?"

"I'll tell you when you get here. There's a train from Penn at 10:03. I'll pick you up at Princeton station. Eat breakfast first." She laughed. "Full disclosure. Ethan and I are living together." She clicked off.

❧ ❧ ❧

"Wow," I said when Becky opened the door to the apartment on William Street. "I pictured a mattress on the floor, dirty socks everywhere, pizza boxes on the counter."

"Left on his own, that's how Ethan would live," Becky said. "Like a homeless person. But he's really sweet."

"Not a description I would have used, but for a big brother, he's OK," I said, and a smile managed to find its way to my face.

The apartment had a narrow entryway. On the wall was a bicycle rack with a woman's bike hanging on it. In the living-dining room was a saggy couch with an African-looking patterned cloth draped over it, a black wood desk with two computer monitors on it, six or eight framed drawings and photos on the walls, and a spotless galley kitchen. The drawings on the wall were small, in chalk or pastel. They were well done: a jagged cityscape, an old man's face, a landscape of plains and trees at night, almost all in black. A photo hung on the wall by the bedroom door: Becky's family on a train going somewhere, happy.

I peeked into the tiny bedroom, which was filled with a king-size bed and two dressers.

"Do you want something to drink? Maybe zombie?" Becky said, with a little smirk.

I stuck out my tongue at her. "Very funny. Show me what you've found," I said.

Becky sat at the desk and patted a chair next to it. "Sit." I sat. She typed on the keyboard and the screens lit up. Becky pointed to the left screen. "Ten days ago, Mikhail Pavluk—Anton's son—opened a bank account and deposited one hundred thousand dollars in it." She pulled up an image of the deposit, a cashier's check, but the signature was illegible. She typed some more, and another cashier's check image appeared, made out to Anthony Garza, Esq., for twelve thousand dollars, also with the same illegible signature. "All

I can tell is that the checks were both drawn from the same account—now closed—at Deutsche Bank in New York," Becky said, leaning back in her chair. "Pavluk's son got some money and hired the lawyer."

Then Becky clicked her mouse, and a document popped up. It was a rental agreement for a house in Miami. "Mikhail moved to Florida two days later." Becky looked me and laughed. "Your mouth is open."

"You're a hacker!" I said.

"Only for friends and family," Becky said. "My degree is in computer science."

We sat together for a minute, me breathing in the faint smell of shampoo and jasmine. Then Becky picked up a manila folder and handed it to me. "Everything I found is in here. Maybe it will help." She held out her hand. "Give me your phone. I'll put in Mikhail's phone number, just in case."

Right. In case I actually wanted to do something. I started to think I maybe I did.

Becky handed back my phone and looked at me. "This is hard for you."

"Yep."

"But you have to decide. If that old man didn't kill your grandparents, then who did? And why?"

That question had been somewhere in my mind since that day in court, but one I hadn't answered. I closed my eyes, seeing that shaky old man reading his confession, seeing the images of the checks to pay off his son, to Garza. It was somebody's story, somebody's plan.

I opened my eyes. Becky was watching me. "At first, I thought maybe it was random, a home invasion," I said. "But then, this Pavluk says he did it out of revenge. I think he's lying."

Becky nodded. "Ethan has told me about the people your grandfather worked for."

"Right. Ukrainian mobsters." I shook my head. "Uncle Teddy loved Grandpa, trusted him. He would never do that."

"Pavluk is Russian. Is there something there?"

I hadn't even thought about that. "There was talk about Russians trying to take over the business."

"You are starting on a path that will not make anything easier. It'll be hard, and at the end, maybe you'll still have no answers."

I closed my eyes again. I saw the firemen bringing those gurneys with the body bags down the front steps. I smelled the smoke.

I was running. Next to me was the fence, someone on the other side five steps ahead, someone I couldn't see. I felt tears again. I opened my eyes. "Where do I start?"

Becky stood up and put her hands on my shoulders. "I think you will figure it out."

I heard the downstairs door and a thump-thump on the stairs. Becky smiled. "It's Ethan. He will be surprised to see you."

Ethan entered wheeling in his bicycle, which he hung on the rack. He turned and saw me and smiled. "Hey, sis." He blushed.

"Hey, bro."

He came into the living room, put his backpack on a chair, and hugged me.

"My straight-arrow brother, living in sin," I said, smiling at the image of Grandma frowning and shaking her head.

He looked a little guilty. "I was going to tell you..." he began.

"It's fine. I have a whole new perspective on you now," I said.

He blushed again and walked over to kiss Becky to hide it. "What's up? Is Becky convincing you to go back to school, I hope?"

Hmmm. Lie, or piss him off? I chose door number two. "Becky's helping me. Somebody killed Grandma and Grandpa, but it wasn't that old guy."

Ethan glared at Becky, and she glared right back. "Your sister is in pain, Ethan."

Ethan sighed, his exasperated-big-brother sigh. "I know. I'm sorry. But Deb, it's over. We know who did it."

I shook my head. "No, we don't. It's what we're supposed to think."

"Listen, little sister. I loved Grandma and Grandpa just as much as you. I've talked to the police, to the DA's office, to everyone. There's nothing. We have to move on. You have to let it go. You need to get—"

I yelled at him, "If I hear the word closure one more time, I'm going to throw something!"

Becky put her arms around Ethan. "You know, Ethan. You know, there are some things…Maybe you want to let go. But they will not let go of you."

Ethan looked at the photo of Becky's family on the wall. He wasn't ready to give up. "I get that. We all need to grieve." He came over to me and put his hand on my arm. "But what you're doing isn't helping. It's making it worse—for you and me."

I yanked my arm away. "What's making it worse is you! Pretending that everything's going to be fine if we just look the other way, if we ignore what's right in front of us!" I grabbed my backpack and headed for the door. "Thanks for the hospitality, Becky."

Ethan came over at the door. "I'm only trying—"

"And failing."

"Let me take you home."

"Forget it. I'll take the train."

Ethan went into the bedroom, slamming the door behind him.

Becky drove me to the train station to catch the 3:38. "Ethan feels very bad too," she said after a while.

"I know. But he doesn't care how I feel," I said.

"You know better than that."

I did, but I was too pissed to admit it.

Becky parked in the tiny train station lot then turned to me. "I'll help you however I can. I think you can do it, Deborah. You have to look for the answers. Perhaps you'll not find them, but don't give up. Don't…" She looked out the car window. If she could have finished her sentence, it would have been something like, "Don't be like me." Becky knew how I felt: a little kid looking into darkness.

I stood under the awning in front of the little nineteenth-century brick depot. A cold wind came down the tracks, blowing the leaves on the trees across from the station. I shivered.

CHAPTER

I woke up on Monday not feeling sorry for myself for a change. I was going to find out who paid Pavluk's lawyer and his son, what the police investigation had discovered, and what—if anything—Uncle Teddy, with all the *orhanizatsiyi's* police connections, knew about it.

After breakfast, I decided to make a call.

"Hello?" a deep gravelly voice replied.

"Is this Mikhail Pavluk, son of Anton Pavluk, formerly residing at 3346 12th Street?" I asked.

Pause. Thinking about it. "What's this about?"

"Mr. Pavluk, my name is Deborah Sokolov. I'm the granddaughter of Viktor and Nadiya Sokolov."

Another pause. "I'm sorry for your loss. What do you want?"

"Did your father ever talk about my grandfather? Did you know about the grudge he held?"

"I haven't talked to my father in six years, Ms. Sokolov. The first I knew of this grudge was when the police called me."

"I understand you received a large sum of money. Do you mind telling me who sent it to you?"

A long pause. I heard a click. I called again and got voicemail. The son wasn't talking. Maybe the father would.

I retrieved Garza's card from the file. When I finally got past his assistant on the phone, I put on my sweetest voice.

"Mr. Garza, I really appreciate all your help, but I need something else. I'd like to visit Mr. Pavluk."

Garza cleared his throat. "That's not a good idea, Ms. Sokolov."

I sniffled. "It's just, I'm trying to move on, you know?" I blew my nose into the phone.

Garza sighed. "I'd have to get special permission...."

"I'd be happy to pay for your trouble." I had who knows how many thousands of dollars in my bank account, plus a credit card.

"It's not possible. I'm very busy."

I cranked out a sob. "Please. Please...I need help to...to get closure." The magic word.

A long pause. I thought I heard another sigh. "I'll call you back in an hour, Ms. Sokolov."

An hour later, Rosa Rodriguez called me. She was Garza's paralegal and would accompany me to Rikers Island, where Pavluk was being held. I gave her my address. An hour after that, a white car pulled up in front of the house. I was coming down the front steps before Rosa Rodriguez—tall, skinny, in a white suit with her hair in braids—was out of the car.

"Hi," I said. "Thanks for doing this."

Rosa nodded, looking away with an expression saying she'd rather be in a dentist's chair than escorting me to Rikers. I slid into the passenger seat. Rosa started the car and we drove off, headed for Ocean Parkway.

Flush with my success in persuading Garza, I decided

to win her over. I leaned forward and sniffled, "I know I'm taking you away from your work, but I really appreciate this. I…just need to see that man, who killed…" Sniffle.

Rosa turned to look at me. "I know. I hope this helps."

Make that a win. I could work up an act.

It was gray and cloudy as we drove over the bridge and through the gate, where a guard checked our IDs and a clipboard.

The red brick North Infirmary looked like a hospital except for the bars on the windows. Rosa decided to stay in the waiting room, patting my shoulder as I went through the door into a green-walled room, with gray plastic tables and chairs.

A door opened, and a guard, supporting Pavluk, came in. Pavluk looked weaker than he'd been in court. He looked at me for a long minute then came and stood opposite me at the table. "What do you want, *malen´ka divchyna*?"

"Little girl" was kind of condescending, but I let it go. I pointed to the chair across from me. He sat down heavily with the guard's help. The guard went off to stand in the corner.

I said, "You didn't kill my grandparents. I want to know who did."

Pavluk snorted. "Of course I did. Viktor killed my brother." He shook his head. "I am sorry about Nadiya. She attacked me, and I defended myself."

"How'd you get to my house? What's the address? Did you drive?"

Pavluk looked at me nervously. He wasn't expecting this. "I don't know what you are talking about."

"Who gave your son a hundred grand?" I leaned over

the table. "Why did you lie? Why did you confess to a crime you didn't commit? Was it the money?"

Pavluk slapped his hand on the table. "Enough! No more questions!" He was really upset. He slid his chair back and almost fell out of it. "Get her out of here! Get her out of here!" The guard hurried over to help him stand up. Pavluk took two steps before his knees buckled. The guard took his arm and they went out.

I had already played my sympathy chip with Rosa. She didn't speak to me on the way back. I called Mikhail Pavluk to hear, "That number has been disconnected and there is no new number."

෨෨෨

Rosa pulled into our driveway behind Grandpa's Buick. As I got out, a black car parked in front of the house started up and drove away.

I warmed up one of Aunt Elena's casseroles, ate, and went to Grandpa's office, sat in his old, squeaky chair to figure out what to do next. I started a list: talk to cops, talk to Uncle Teddy.

My phone rang. I recognized Garza's cell number. I was expecting him to ask how it went with Pavluk.

"Ms. Sokolov. I...I'm sorry. I shouldn't have agreed to your visit."

"It's OK. I want to thank you, even though Pavluk didn't help me much," I replied.

"No, no. I...You can't...Don't call me anymore. I can't talk to you." His voice sounded like it was being squeezed in a juicer. This was a frightened guy.

"What's wrong? What happened?" I heard a click. I called him back but got voicemail.

Interesting. Pavluk's son canceled his phone, and somebody scared the crap out of Garza. I must be doing something right.

৵৵৵

The 60th Precinct cop shop was on 8th and Ocean, across from the El. The rattle of trains echoed faintly through the building on this Tuesday morning. At the front desk, a bald, blue-uniformed sergeant was reading the *Post*.

"Can I help you, young lady?" he asked.

"I'd like to speak to Detective O'Malley," I replied.

"And you are?"

"Deborah Sokolov."

"Take a seat. I'll see if he's available." I sat on a hard wooden bench. He picked up the phone and spoke to someone.

After a couple of minutes, I heard a voice: "Deborah?" I turned to see Boris Sirko, a neighborhood kid who'd joined the NYPD a couple of years ago. He was in his twenties, tall, blond, with big blue eyes, and looking cool in his uniform. I'd had a crush on him when he was a teenager and I was ten.

Boris came over. "I am so sorry about Viktor and Nadiya."

I nodded a thank you. "That's why I'm here. I need answers to some questions." I looked over my shoulder. The desk cop was reading about the real housewives of Long Island. I took the manila folder out of my backpack and handed it to him. "I want to talk to Detective O'Malley, who investigated my grandparents' deaths."

Boris flipped through the pages then beckoned me to

follow. We went through a door marked Squad Room and into a high-ceilinged room that smelled of burned coffee. It was filled with ten or so desks, some with men and women seated at them, going through paperwork or typing on computers. He introduced me to Detective O'Malley, a TV version of a cop. He was in his fifties, with rimless glasses sliding down his bulbous nose, a potbelly, and bushy eyebrows. Boris took him aside for a few whispered words then said goodbye to me. "My patrol partner's waiting."

Detective O'Malley took me to his desk. Over his shoulder, he said, "I never met your grandparents, but I heard they were good people." We sat. "What do you need, honey?"

"I didn't see any interviews with people on the block in the police report. My next-door neighbor heard a car—"

O'Malley held up a hand. "Lemme tell you. Before we even got started, this Pavluk came into the station, turned himself in. He confessed to the crime. A team went to his apartment and found the gun. Pavluk's prints were on it, ballistics confirmed—you know the details."

"You never talked to the neighbors?" I asked.

"What for? We had the guy."

"You never checked out the car that my neighbor, Mr. Krasny, heard driving off?"

"Like I said, honey, we had the guy. Case closed."

"How'd Pavluk get to our house? He lived a mile or so away. And it's a mile from our house to here. He can barely walk."

O'Malley shrugged. "Maybe he took a cab." He looked at me, another raised eyebrow. "What're you after, honey?"

"Honey" was getting a little annoying, but O'Malley was like an uncle who says non-PC stuff that the family agrees to ignore. I managed a tiny smile, trying out my sympathy chip. "People keep telling me I need closure, that I need to move on. This is…is hard, but it helps."

O'Malley raised a bushy eyebrow. "Hmmm. That sounds like BS. You don't think this Pavluk did it, do ya, honey?"

He made me smile. "You got me." I paused, wondering whether or not to say more. I cleared my throat. "I visited Pavluk. At Rikers. He was sick and weak. I can't see him doing what he says he did."

O'Malley smiled. "Well, you got brass ones, I'll give you that." He looked over his shoulder, then at me. "I gotta say, it was a little strange." He leaned forward. "Pedro—my partner—and I were canvassing your block Friday morning when we got a call that Pavluk had turned himself in. We put the guy into an interview room, started asking questions, you know, getting his statement. Two minutes later, the Brooklyn ADA came in and took Pavluk. 'We've got this, O'Malley,' he said." O'Malley leaned back in his chair. "Anyway, before I knew it, Pavluk's off to Rikers." He shrugged. "Whaddya gonna do?"

"How about questioning him?" I asked.

"It's outta my hands, honey," he replied. O'Malley looked around the squad room, nodding his head in the direction of a glass-walled office with Captain Mushin written on the door. "You wanna know more, talk to the captain."

I thanked O'Malley and went over Captain Mushin's office, but he wasn't there. I spoke to the gray-haired lady sitting at a nearby desk. "I'm Deborah Sokolov." I took a notepad off her desk, which annoyed her, and wrote down my phone number. "Please have the captain call me. It's about the Policeman's Widow's Society," which was something I'd just made up.

❧❧❧

I was coming back from a run when I turned the corner onto Second Street and saw a police car in front of the house. Coming to bust me? I didn't think so.

A skinny cop with some gold bars on his blue jacket got out of the back seat. I stopped on the sidewalk. "Ms. Sokolov? I'm Captain Mushin. I understand you wanted to speak to me."

"Yeah. It's about my grandparents' murders."

He smiled. Not a nice smile. "Oh, I thought it was about the Policeman's Widow's Society, which doesn't exist." He pointed to the house. "Maybe we should go in and talk."

"We're good here," I replied.

Mushin leaned back against the cop car, his arms folded. "Fine. You're going to have to stop bothering my officers about a case that's already been solved. Pavluk confessed, he's been sent to prison."

"Except he's not the guy," I said.

Mushin unfolded one arm to wave my words away. "You don't know anything."

"I know that somebody paid Pavluk's son a hundred thousand bucks. I know that that same somebody paid the lawyer."

Mushin's face got red. His waving hand turned into a pointing finger that he shook at me. "Stop interfering in police work!"

For a second, I thought he didn't know about those payoffs. Then it struck me: maybe he *did* know but was surprised that I did, too. O'Malley's puzzlement about how his investigation had been shut down started to make sense.

I turned to go and noticed Boris in the driver's seat of the cop car. He didn't turn his head to look at me, even though I waved.

I left red-faced Mushin standing on the sidewalk and went in the house.

OK: Garza, Pavluk's son, and now Mushin. Maybe I was on to something. Cops are friendly with Uncle Teddy, so maybe with the Russians too?

I texted Becky about my talk with Pavluk and Mushin's visit. A second later, she texted back: *You're doing something right. Be careful. Cops might not be your friends.*

ॐॐॐ

After lunch, I decided to get Grandpa's stuff out of the garage and bring it inside. I was strangely beginning to feel good about myself. Maybe I could overcome my Ukrainian gloom.

As I lifted open garage door, the faint, lingering odor of smoke hit me, and the memory came back. The smoke-filled house, the EMTs bringing out two gurneys…

I pushed the memory away.

A half-dozen empty plastic bins were stacked on the cement floor, all neatly labeled: Living Room, Dining Room, Hall Closet. Most of the stuff had already been put back in the house.

I found one bin labeled Office and opened it. Grandpa's old books—a history of the Ukraine, a dictionary, his tattered Bible—were on top. Grandpa's laptop wasn't there, but he never used it for bookkeeping. "Too many people can change things," he'd told me. "I copy the numbers into the office computer to keep Teo happy."

Under the laptop were a ring of keys and the metal box with the Nagant. The ring held keys to the Buick, the Nagant box, our house, Grandpa's office, the basement room at East-West where I'd learned to shoot, and another small silver key I didn't recognize. At the bottom of the box were a few papers, crisped around the edges. I leafed through them. Most were bills and letters from businesses to East-West Imports.

I picked up the bin and put it on a stack of newspapers that was kind of leaning against the garage wall then put the stuff back in.

I picked up the bin and the newspaper pile fell over, revealing a locked black metal box that looked a hundred years old. I'd never seen it before. I took the key ring and tried the silver key. It worked. I opened the lid.

Inside the box was Grandpa's green eight by ten ledger.

I sat on the fallen stack of papers. I opened the ledger, and a memory came back: Grandpa at his desk, going through stacks of paper, entering figures in the book in his tiny handwriting. I closed my eyes. I was eight or nine, looking over his shoulder as he wrote. The pendulum clock ticked away on the wall by the door. Behind us was the bookshelf, filled with books in Ukrainian, an ancient world atlas, black-and-white family photos on the wall.

What's this, Grandpa?

This is an invoice.

What's an invoice?

When we buy something, the seller provides us with a bill, or invoice, showing the money we owe. I put the amount in my book and the date it was paid.

Stop bothering your grandfather, Deborah. Grandma's voice, as she stood at the door.

She's not bothering me, Nadiya. She's learning something. That's what school is for.

I opened my eyes, wet with tears. Damn Becky.

Another memory came back: Uncle Teddy's angry voice.

Someone is stealing from me!

Grandpa's voice, calm, assured.

I told you this months ago. You chose to ignore it.

And then Grandpa took out his ledger—this ledger—to show Uncle Teddy. He'd known something was wrong and that the entries he made every night would show it, would prove that someone was stealing from the *orhanizatsiyi*. The next night he and Grandma were murdered, and their killer set the fire. The killer thought the ledger was destroyed as well.

I leafed through the ledger, turning pages to the most recent dates. Starting in January, several of the entries had weird symbols in the margins written in Grandpa's spidery script. There were dozens of them, through February, March, April, and May. The last one was May 14, the night my grandparents were murdered. There were nine different entries, repeating over and over:

ꝓꝋꙆꙅ ꙅꙆꙆꞃħℙ ꙅ·ħ₄ꙅꙆꙆꞃħ ⱣꞃħꙆꙆꙂ·ꙅꙆꙛꙅꙆꙆꞃħ ꝓ ꙅ·ħꙆꙆ Ᵽ꙰₄ꙅⱣꙆꙆ ⱣꙂꙆꙆꙅ

₄ꙅꙛꙅꙆꙆꞃħℙ ꙆꞃħꙆꙆꙆꙆꙆꙛꙅ

I can read Cyrillic. This wasn't it. It was some other language, or maybe a code.

I took a picture and messaged it to Becky.

I put the green ledger back in the box and locked it. I carried it and the box with the Nagant into the house.

Criminals and politicians—who are sometimes the same

people—hide dirty money in their refrigerators. I should hide my secret. I took out one of Voly's frozen dinners: veggies, mashed potatoes, and "Salisbury steak," aka hamburger. Debating whether or not to actually eat it, I took the microwave-safe plastic tray out of the box, put the ledger and translations in it, and stuffed it in the back of the freezer, behind Aunt Elena's and Mrs. Krasny's casseroles. Then I went to bed.

❧❧❧

I called the precinct to talk to Detective O'Malley, but he wasn't in. The cop on the phone wouldn't give me O'Malley's cell phone number.

The next morning, my phone buzzed me awake. It was Becky. "It's an old alphabet, called Glagolitic. I know someone who might figure out the meaning. Meet me at Canal Street Station."

"It's seven in the morning!" I whined. "High school dropouts don't have to get up this early."

"If you take the 8:36, you can be there by 9:20," she said, ignoring my whining. "Call when you're on your way."

Becky waved at me as I came through the gate with the ledger tucked in my backpack. We hugged briefly.

"I didn't have breakfast," I said. "You want to get something?"

"I'm famished," she said, nodding.

"Most people say 'hungry,'" I teased her.

"Princeton. The High Council," she laughed as we rode up the escalator, our arms around one another.

"Most of the notes are in Ukrainian and English," I said as Becky looked over the ledger pages at our table in the crowded restaurant. "But here, starting in January, Grandpa started writing in this weird language."

Becky ran her fingers down a column. "They're not on every entry," she said, pointing to a page from March. "Just some of them. What's this?" she asked, her finger on an entry from March 24.

I leaned over to look: *papir dlya pryntera*. "Printer paper," I told her.

"You know, eighteen hundred dollars' worth of paper seems like a lot," Becky said, her eyebrow raised. "Is your family in the printing business?"

"No, at least not that I know about." I was a little defensive about my Ukrainian gangster connection. "Grandpa put the ledger in a metal box and hid it in our garage. That's the only reason it wasn't burned."

"If your grandfather went to all this trouble—coded entries, keeping the book safe—he knew something was wrong."

"I figured that out," I said.

Becky got up. "Let's go find out what it means."

&ono&ono&ono

This part of the East Village had once been a Ukrainian neighborhood, but most of the Ukrainians had left, except for a few old people tangled in their roots. Chinatown and gentrification were squeezing out the last bit of the Ukraine.

The Holy Trinity Ukrainian Church on Broome Street took me back to my childhood, and it also took me back to the time I ran away from the funeral at that other church. Becky and I walked up the stone stairs, and I stood on the top step, not moving. Becky took my arm and pulled me inside.

The church smelled of candlewax, incense, and old age. It was empty except for two bent-over women, all in black, scarves on their heads, sitting in the pews.

Becky said, "Wait here," and went off. I walked up and down the aisles, tried doors, peeked behind the ornate front wall with its pictures of saints, martyrs, and angels. I opened the door to a confessional, went in, and sat on the hard wooden seat. I'd last been in one of these claustrophobic booths when I was twelve, at Grandma's insistence, because I was having trouble with a teacher and not doing my homework. A promise to say a few Hail Marys and obey my grandparents and my teachers, and I was forgiven.

Just then, a young, smiling, slightly chubby bearded man in a t-shirt and shorts poked his head in. "Let me change, and I'll be right back." Becky was standing behind him.

Embarrassed, I jumped out of the confessional. "No, no. I'm not here for…I need some help…" My tongue stumbled over my teeth.

"That's what I'm here for," he said. "I'm Father Andriy. Call me Andy."

My clichéd picture of Ukrainian priests—old men with white beards, bushy eyebrows, and fierce glares channeling the wrath of God—vanished. "Not that kind of help. I have something I need translated," I finally managed to spit out.

"Yes. Rebecca emailed me. She taught a computer class I took at NYU last summer. Come to my office," he said and went off. We followed.

The priest's dusty, wood-paneled study smelled like a library, which it kind of was. The walls were lined with shelves filled with books: old, leatherbound ones and newer paperbacks.

Father Andy moved some papers off a chair and waved his hand. "Sorry about the mess. I kind of forget about it until I get embarrassed when visitors come." We sat.

"Oh, and apologies for my unpriestly attire," he said, pointing to his t-shirt. "I was cleaning up some trash in the back."

Andy pulled two pages from a pile on his desk. "Glagolitic is the earliest known form of Cyrillic, from the tenth century in Eastern Europe. I had to do some research," he said, waving to a teetering pile of books on a shelf behind him. He swiveled in his chair and took out one of the old, leatherbound volumes. He opened it, and there were the funny characters. "Your grandfather was a very educated man." That was something I never knew.

Andy leaned back and pulled another sheet of paper from the pile. "Here's the translation." He put the sheet in front of me. "There are nine Glagolitic notations. Is that all you have?"

I nodded. "The words are repeated several times in my Grandpa's book."

Andy leaned over his desk to point at the entries, and Becky and I leaned forward. "I skipped the Cyrillic and translated them to the Latin alphabet—what we use to write in English."

ΠϽΠΠБЯ = *Petro* = *Peter*

ЯΠΠrhP = *Ivan* = *James*

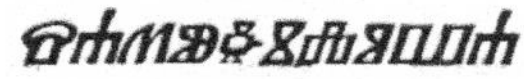

ΘrhΛ1Ж♀ЯⴔЯΠΠrh = *Samuel*

♀rh<ЯΠΠrh = *Jacob* = *John*

Π♀rhΠΠ Θ�Λ♂ΘΠΠ ΘϽΛ1♀ = *P'yat' shist' semy* = *Five Six Seven*

<ЯⴔЯΛ1rhP = *Koloman* = ?

ΛΛrhΠΠⴓⴓ8♀ = *Matviy* = *Matthew*

"The names could be people your grandfather knew. But they're also books of the Bible. Matthew is a New Testament book, as are Ivan and Jacob, James and John." Andy said. "The numbers five, six and seven, I don't know."

"What about Koloman?" Becky asked.

Andy grinned. "That was a head-scratcher. The only Koloman I found at first was a twentieth-century Austrian artist, Koloman Moser. Thirty pages in Google! His artwork's for sale on eBay. But I did some more research and found that Koloman was the first king of Hungary, in the eleventh century." Andy shrugged. "But I don't know what that could mean for your grandfather." Andy handed the pages to me. "I hope you find what you're looking for," he said.

All I knew for sure was that whatever these entries meant, Grandpa didn't want anyone knowing. I thanked Father Andy and we left, the smell of incense lingering in my nostrils, the memory lingering in my brain, poking at me. I needed some fresh air.

"Now what?" Becky asked as we walked to the subway.

I didn't know. Every step I took was leading me down a path next to a fence I couldn't see over, and someone was on the other side of the fence.

৵৵৵

I had turned off the Parkway onto Ocean View going back to the house on Second when I saw flashing blue and red lights in my rear-view mirror.

I pulled over to the curb. In my side mirror, I saw a tall, skinny silhouette get out of the cop car. I sighed. It was Boris. I cranked down the window and put on my nicest smile.

"Hey, Boris. I don't think I was speeding. Do I have a taillight out?"

Boris held out his hand. "Driver's license and registration, please."

Oh. All formal. I handed him my license and fumbled in the glove compartment for the registration. "Here you go, Boris…er, Officer Sirko."

He pretended to look at my stuff then handed them back to me, leaning his head in the window. I thought he wanted to kiss me—my preteen dream come true. "You have to stop what you're doing."

I was frustrated and tired of playing dumb. "Look, we both know the old guy didn't kill my grandparents. How long are you going to be the messenger boy for whoever did kill them? Do they pay you well?" There. I'd said it. The shit will hit the fan.

Boris stood up and looked down the street, then slammed his hand on the roof of my car. "Dammit! You have no idea of what you're getting into! Stop being so stubborn!"

"It's my nature, Officer," I said, smiling sweetly.

Boris took a deep breath. "I hear things at the precinct. O'Malley got transferred for talking to you."

"I'm sorry about that," I said, and I was.

"After your visit, two Russian-looking guys in suits came to Mushin's office and," he looked up and down the street again, "they were arguing. I heard 'Sokolov.'"

"Russians in suits? So what?"

Boris looked up and down the street again. "There are rumors. The Russian syndicate is moving in."

I remembered the conversation I'd overheard at Uncle Teddy's apartment.

Boris leaned in closer. "They have friends in the police." He put his hand on my shoulder. "I want you to be safe. You have to stop this, what you're doing."

I took a deep breath, dialing it down. "OK. Thanks for the heads-up. I promise not to bother the cops anymore. I don't want you to get into trouble. No more visits to mobster-puppet Mushin or Pavluk, who didn't kill my grandparents."

As Boris turned to go, he said, "I'm your friend, Deborah," which made me feel guilty.

That night I had a dream about a wolf pacing in the living room, on one side of a wooden fence with someone on the other side.

❧❧❧

I woke up when phone rang. It was night. I looked over at my clock. 2:30. I answered, noticing that the number was blocked. "Hello?" No answer. "Hello?" I heard noise in the background, like cars maybe. "Listen, prank calls work best if you actually have a prank." Silence. "Nice talking to you." I clicked off.

An hour later, my phone rang again. This time whoever it was clicked off when I answered. I turned off my phone.

In the morning, I made another copy of the ledger entries and translations. I sat in Grandpa's office and studied them. Peter. Samuel. Five Six Seven. Koloman. Matthew. I tried lining up the first letters. I tried the numeric equivalents of the letters. I tried saying them out loud.

What the hell does this mean, Grandpa?

Grandpa didn't answer. After another useless hour, I put the scans and the ledger in the Hungry Man box.

෧෧෧

I had a late dinner at Wing's—best Mongolian barbeque on Long Island—and walked back home. As I walked up Second Street, I saw that the house was dark. I'd left both my bedroom light and the living room lamp on. I stopped at the Buick and retrieved the Nagant from the trunk then tiptoed up the front steps.

Someone smarter than me would have dialed 911. Someone even a little less stupid would have at least not gone in.

I smelled cigarettes when I opened the front door. In movies, the victim always calls out, "Hello? Who's there?" letting whoever is after her (it's always a her) know she's alone and vulnerable. Even when I was little, I knew that was dumb. I listened for two minutes but heard no sound. Partly pissed and mostly scared, I took a breath or two. Tiptoeing on the wooden floor, revolver in my hand, avoiding the floorboards that creaked, I went in. I waited twenty minutes, until the old pendulum clock chimed, but heard nothing.

I turned on the kitchen lights. An angry or desperate searcher had stomped through, throwing things on the linoleum, dumping drawers. The refrigerator and freezer doors were open, but the box still had the ledger and scans. The searcher hadn't seen the same movies.

I took off my shoes and went upstairs, listened. Nothing. I went to my room and turned on the light.

The mattress was dumped upside down on the floor, the desk drawers were pulled out and emptied. My trophy shelf had been tipped over, books and papers scattered everywhere. Dirty laundry was dumped on the floor.

I went into my grandparents' bedroom, where I hadn't been since they were killed. Everything was flung onto the floor. I straightened their black-and-white wedding picture on the wall.

I picked up a framed photograph that had resided on Grandma's side table. The glass was cracked. Grandpa, Grandma, my parents, Ethan with his thumb in his mouth, and me in my mothers' arms on the tiny lawn in front of Grandma's rosebushes.

The bed cover is wrinkled. Pull it tight.

I know, Grandma. I know.

In the living room, the couch cushions were on the floor, the chair Grandma used to sit in turned over. Her Bible, which always sat on the wobbly table next to her chair, was open face-down on the floor. I picked it up and put it on the table.

In Grandpa's office, all the desk drawers were open. The few East-West Imports folders, papers, and invoices , from companies using the Cyrillic alphabet, were scattered on the floor. Red-hot anger or something was in my brain, maybe hot enough to melt the glass shards.

I cleaned the house—sweeping, setting furniture right, dumping broken glass and crumpled papers into the kitchen trash bin.

Gotta feed Dobby. I got a can of cat food out of the cabinet. I opened the can into a bowl and took it out to the back porch. One of the glass panes in the back door was broken; that's how the intruder had entered. It was dark, and I stepped out, calling, "Here, Dobby, here, Dobby." My foot hit something soft. In the dim light from the street, I saw Dobby sprawled and hanging halfway off the step. Her throat had been cut. The porch was soaked in her blood. Her mouth was open, her sharp teeth bared in a death grimace, a useless warning.

I crouched down and petted her dead body, already cold and stiff. I felt tears coming, but I swallowed them back. I got a shovel from the garage and dug a hole next to our back fence in the little vegetable garden Grandma had planted two months ago. Squash, tomatoes, and corn were dying or dead.

I got a towel to cover Dobby. As I put my hands under her to pick her up, I felt something sticking out from under her. I turned her body over. A switchblade knife was stuck in her side, pinning a piece of paper to her bloody fur. I pulled out the knife and turned the paper over. A photo. Ethan and Becky walking down a street, holding hands.

So much for melting the fragments. They came back in bunches. Anger disappeared, and pain filled my head until it was like a balloon about to burst. But then it was around me, surrounding me, and I was in the middle of it, squeezed and crushed in a trash compactor.

ই৵ই৵ই৵

I woke up and realized it was Sunday. Then I realized I was angry again. Somebody killed Grandma and Grandpa, trashed my house, and threatened Ethan and Becky. Somebody killed my cat.

I had coffee from the new coffeemaker and ate a bowl of cereal. I put the Nagant into the Buick's trunk and drove to East-West Imports.

The basement still smelled of gunpowder. The table still faced the stacks of newspapers where the targets still hung. The lights still hummed their song.

I opened the metal box and took out the revolver and the cleaning kit. The gun was clean, but I cleaned it again anyway, checking the cylinder, tightening the screws with a tiny screwdriver. Tears came to my throat, to the back of my eyes, but I ignored them. Grandpa was looking over my shoulder.

Loaded or unloaded, Deborah?

Always loaded unless I check it to make sure.

The effective range?

Fifty feet, allowing for weather.

Only if you are good. Twenty-five feet is better.

The paper target's concentric rings blurred and dissolved into faces, people I didn't know, people who killed my grandparents. I put every shot inside the nine ring, a dozen or so in the red bullseye. I was really good at this, maybe not so good at dealing with other stuff. When I'd finished, I sat down at the rickety wooden table and cleaned the gun, putting scrubbing the inside of the barrel with the bronze wire brush, then putting oil on a fresh white patch, threading it through the eyelet in the rod, and running it through the barrel until it came out clean. When I was finished, I reloaded, carefully putting the rounds in the gun's cylinder.

Look, Grandpa. I did good. I cleaned it perfectly.

Afterward I locked up the basement room and went outside. Voly was at the top of the basement stairs. "I heard some shooting," he said.

I held up the Nagant in its case. "Just practicing."

"I haven't seen you in a month," he said, his bushy eyebrow raised.

I shrugged. "I had to take some time off."

He nodded. "It was hard for you." He looked at me. "But you look well."

"Come to the house."

"I have work to do."

"I'll make lunch," I said.

He tilted his head, baring his neck tattoo, a Ukrainian cross. "I'll order pizza from Sam's."

"I can cook!"

Voly made a "yeah, right" face.

"Fine. I'll nuke Aunt Elena's casserole." That got him.

"Half an hour." He turned and went up the stairs to the office.

I put the Nagant in the trunk and sat on a railroad tie at the edge of the parking lot, looking out over the river. It was already turning hot and muggy, a New York summer.

I wanted to be on that big boat with the bright yellow sail heading out into Long Island Sound.

But I was here.

CHAPTER

I was taking Elena's casserole out of the microwave when
the doorbell rang.

Voly came in, almost having to duck to avoid bumping his head on the door frame. He followed me into the
dining room, and I served lunch.

After we'd finished putting dishes in the dishwasher, we
went into the living room. "I've got something to show you."
I went into Grandpa's office, brought back the ledger and
Father Andy's translations, and sat next to him on the new
red couch. "Check this out."

Voly opened the ledger and his eyes widened. "This was
Viktor's," he said, looking at me. "Teo, everyone, they think it
was destroyed in—" He stopped.

"In the fire," I finished for him. "It's OK. You can say it. I
think it's Grandpa's code about the money missing from the
business. It's what Uncle Teddy came to see Grandpa about."

Voly picked up the ledger. "I have to show this to Teo. It
might mean something to him."

I grabbed it away and stood up. "No! You're not taking
it! You can't have it! Nobody can have it!"

Voly stood up, his six-foot-whatever frame towering

over me, his broad shoulders blocking the light. He could break me like a matchstick. But he wouldn't. I looked up at him.

"What's in this has something to do with why Grandma and Grandpa were murdered," I explained.

"Pavluk…" he began.

"Yeah, right, Pavluk," I said. "He didn't do it. Somebody paid off his family, somebody bought his confession. For a hundred thousand dollars."

Voly, not a guy with the big facial expressions, or even the little ones, opened his mouth and closed it again. "How do you know?"

I told him about my visits to the cops and Pavluk. I showed him the bloody photo of Ethan and Becky. "It was on a knife that was stuck in my dead cat."

Voly sat down again, slumping on the couch. He put his head in his hands. After a few seconds, he looked up. "When Teo found me, I was on the streets, eating out of dumpsters, sleeping in alleys. He raised me like one of his own, like another son." Voly turned to look at me. "Teo loved Viktor like a brother."

More to comfort him, I said, "I don't think Uncle Teddy had anything to do with my grandparents' murders." I told Voly about Uncle Teddy's Thursday night visit with Grandpa. "On Friday, somebody, not Pavluk, murdered my grandparents."

After a minute, Voly leaned back on the couch, putting his finger on his chin. "Olek has been talking to the Russians. He wants to make deals with them, to work with them. Teo and Olek have been arguing about it."

"The Russians," I said. "But I have nothing, no proof."

Voly stood up. "Keep those records safe. And keep yourself safe."

Voly walked to the door then turned to me. "One day, when you were eight, you, Ethan, Olek, and a neighborhood boy were playing in your front yard. Olek was teasing your brother, pushing him around, knocking him to the grass. You jumped on Olek's back and started hitting him. I had to pull you off and stop Olek before he broke your nose." He opened the door. "I'll look into this. Be careful, Deborah. You are brave, but you are also stubborn and stupid."

"I'm not eight years old anymore, Voly," I replied.

I'd done nothing, found nothing, yet someone wanted me to stop, someone wanted me to be afraid. Maybe the only reason I wasn't dead was because the killer didn't know what I knew or if I'd told someone else.

What if it was Voly? Voly could not have done this. He would not, I argued with myself. He was my friend, my protector.

What if it was Uncle Teddy?

What if it was a random home invader and cat killer who just happened to have a photo of my brother and his girlfriend?

Thoughts swirled around like the eggs Grandma used to whip up with her hand mixer for Sunday breakfast. I knew one thing for sure: If I kept on doing what I was doing, my brother and Becky were in danger. If I kept on poking around, they might die. I couldn't tell Becky. She'd say, "Ethan and I will be fine. You go, girl." Telling Ethan was number one on a list of really bad ideas.

I went inside and sat in the dark at the dining room table. I closed my eyes and put my cheek on the old, cool wooden surface. After maybe a minute or two, I could hear faintly Grandma and Grandpa talking to each other.

Anna skazala, shcho vony dodayut' nomer v zadniy chastyni dlya Sashi i yiyi novoho dytyny. Anna said they're adding a room to their house for Sasha and the new baby.

Anatoliy mozhe dopomohty yim. Ya budu nazyvaty yoho. Anatoliy can help them. I will call him.

I opened my eyes. In my mind I could see them sitting in their usual places at the table. Grandpa spoke: *Vovchytsya. The she-wolf, Deborah. The she-wolf.*

I yelled, "There is no she-wolf. The she-wolf is dead! Like you!" They were gone. I was yelling at an empty room.

৯৯৯

Early the next morning, I went running. Down Second Street to Ocean, under the El, as delivery vans and random three a.m. trucks honked at me. I ran and ran and ran and ran. Mingled tears and sweat evaporated.

I ran. My legs loosened; the muscles did their work. I ran past a construction site with a wooden fence that I couldn't see over. I ran down Ocean to West End, to Emmons and then Knapp. I ran some more, the slap-slap of my running shoes on the concrete matching the beats of my heart. I felt the wind in my face—no, I made the wind, I created the wind, by running.

I ran. I ran to the Marsh Trail, which I hadn't been on since middle school, smelling the salt, the decay of dead fish. I ran off the trail into the trees and brush, branches slapping at my legs. Down a hill, stumbling, almost falling, I ran into the water, up to my ankles, up to my knees. I waded deeper, mud swirling like clouds around my waist. Salt stung my legs where branches had cut them. I moved forward, the mud holding me, pulling at my feet. Deeper and deeper, now up to my chest, up to my chin, nothing and no one but me and the smell, and in the distance, green trees and a faint scattering of stars overhead. I bent down and sank beneath the scummy green water. I opened my eyes but there was only darkness. I stood it as long as I could but then pushed myself to the surface, breathing again. I stood up in the water, getting cold.

෨෨෨

The sun was coming up when I got back to the house. I went to the back door and stripped, dumping my clothes in the trash can next to the back stairs, which were stained with Dobby's blood.

I showered and changed into another pair of jeans and a sweatshirt, found my sandals under the bed. I opened the door and peeked into Grandma and Grandpa's room, looking for ghosts. They weren't there. I said goodbye.

I drove to the Avenue Salon. "I need a new me," I told the red-headed hair stylist. She nodded in agreement, and I felt a little insulted. An hour later, my stringy blonde hair was washed and trimmed in what the stylist called "a stacked bob." I had my bristly eyebrows waxed, got my raggedy nails done by a smiling manicurist, said no thanks to another woman who approached me with her hands full of eyeliner, lipstick, and blush. I almost didn't recognize myself when I looked in the mirror. Looking good on the outside, anyway.

I googled "fake ids new york" on my phone, then drove to Roosevelt Avenue in Queens. The third kid I asked directed me to QuikShot Photo. An hour and a hundred fifty bucks later, I had a brand-new social security card and driver's license, and I was now twenty-one-year-old Deborah Sturm.

At the Chase Bank in Park Slope, as Deborah Sokolov, I withdrew fifty thousand dollars from the education fund in a cashier's check. I told the bank manager that it was for school. Ethan would cut me off. I didn't care.

At the Chase Bank in Gravesend, as Deborah Sturm, I opened a new account, deposited the fifty grand, and got a brand-new debit card.

Back at the house, I got the ledger from the freezer, packed it into the box with Grandpa's revolver, stuffed it and my bathroom gear into my backpack, then went out and locked the front door. I breathed a goodbye to Grandpa and Grandma's ghosts, walked down to Ocean, and grabbed the Q to the city.

&⁓&⁓&⁓

A pair of Louboutin combat boots, Joe's Jeans, a Marc Jacobs knit top, some nice earrings, and a black Coach bag later, I looked in store windows on Houston Street and admired myself. Shrapnel still floated around somewhere in a corner of my brain, but I was going to shrink the fragments into something manageable. I had always wanted to get better grades than Ethan and run faster than Brianna. But that's not who I was. I was the runner-up, second place, the red ribbon, the smaller trophy. That didn't matter anymore. Now I was a new Deborah.

All the shopping had made me hungry, but I looked too cool to grab a slice from a corner pizza place. I found a café and had some onion soup and, thanks to my new ID, a glass of wine.

A bar on Mott Street had music, so I stopped in. It was early and not too crowded. I found a table and ordered wine. The oldies playlist was from a sound system, but the waitress said the band would be in later.

Later arrived, and so did the eighties glam rock cover band, which was pretty good, and although I'm not a fan of eighties rock, I liked the Bowie tribute. After that, I walked over to Broadway and checked into a boutique hotel. I slept for ten hours and ordered room service for breakfast.

❧❧❧

The next day, I got a six-month lease on a crummy, no-bedroom first-floor apartment on Elizabeth Street for $2,000 a month. I walked up to the corner, and there was the Holy Trinity church Becky and I had visited to talk to Father Andy. I had to laugh at myself. No matter how fast I ran, my Ukrainian DNA caught up to me.

I'd left Brighton Beach behind. I spent the week and a couple grand buying furniture and dishes and more clothes. I texted Ethan that I needed some time to myself then called Mrs. Krasny and asked her to please pick up the mail. Ethan called me and left an angry voicemail. "I've taken you off the account, Deborah. What the hell are you doing with that money?" I didn't call back.

I met my neighbor Ian, who lived upstairs in a larger and nicer apartment and had a hedge fund manager boyfriend. He sported a topknot, a dangling earring in his right ear, a tiny beard, sunglasses, and a stingy-brim hat, which he told me was the official hipster uniform.

One afternoon, while watching the Yankees overwhelm the Red Sox on my new TV—his choice, not mine—and eating deli sandwiches in my living room-kitchen-bedroom, I asked him what he did for a living.

Ian raised his finger. "Glad you asked." He went out, and I heard him on the stairs. A few minutes later, he came back holding a baggie. "I'm your friendly neighborhood dealer." He sat down next to me on the couch. "Want to try some? You'll forget all your problems."

"Yeah, right," I said. "You're just being a good salesman."

He smiled at me. "I am not kidding."

My first and last experience with what I'd thought was marijuana was in the eighth grade. It turned out to be oregano, and I hadn't tried anything stronger than Advil or a glass of wine since. Even though I'd never tell him, Ethan was kind of my role model growing up: straight arrow. He never even drank beer. I shook my head. "I don't think so."

"You mind if I partake?" Ian asked.

"I don't care."

He pulled out a glass pipe, crunched some green buds between his fingers into the pipe bowl, and lit it. The pipe flamed, and sweet-smelling smoke rose into the air. Ian leaned back on the couch with a sigh.

He offered the pipe. "You sure?"

What the hell. I was the new Deborah. I took a tiny puff and coughed and coughed. Ian laughed. My body tingled. This was good. I took three more puffs, feeling the tingling grow, my body vibrating like a tuning fork.

"Hey, hey. Take it easy," Ian warned.

Suddenly I was floating above my body, looking down at

me lying back on the couch, looking up at me gazing down at me. This was not oregano.

Ian watched me with that smile. "See?" he said.

My brain tried to get my mouth to speak, but it wouldn't. From my ceiling perch, I watched Ian take the pipe from my hand and puff on it. He leaned back, looked up, and smiled at me.

I finally croaked out, "This is…is…something else."

Ian grinned. "A little something called salvia mixed in. Makes it more intense."

I closed my eyes and floated around the ceiling for I don't know how long. When I woke up or came to, I was back in my body, and Ian was snoring. The buzz was wearing off, but every nerve in my body was singing a happy tune. I closed my eyes again, checking on the sharp things in my head. They were still there in a corner of my brain, but I didn't care. I could manage them, control them. Good news.

ชิชิชิ

Monday night, I went to Captain Nemo, a club Ian and his hedge fund significant other (whose name I couldn't remember) had told me about. It was crowded and, despite the mayor's orders, cloudy with smoke. I'd already been a few times. Some new band was playing this time, loud and angry.

A stringy-haired guy came over and held out his closed fists. "Pick one."

I shook my head nicely. "No thanks."

"Come on, babe, you're gonna love this."

"I love this," I replied, holding up my drink, which was

vodka and orange juice, I think.

I was in the only chair at my table, but he shoved me over and squeezed in next to me. Annoying. He opened his fists to reveal two green-and-white capsules. He popped one in his mouth. "Really, try it. It's a whole new world."

"In my world, no means no, asshole," I said, shifting my hip hard so he staggered off his perch. "Besides, look at you. A fashion disaster. No-name jeans, sneakers from the thrift store, a bad haircut. And you have awful breath."

For some reason, he didn't take well to my critique. "What a cunt!" he yelled at me.

He grabbed my arm. I pulled back, but his grip was pretty firm. I looked around the club for help.

"Let go," I said, and he did. I lost my balance (probably because it was my third drink) and fell to the floor, banging my head on the edge of the chair. "Ow!" I yelled.

The bartender came over and helped me up. I was pissed. "What kind of lowlifes do you let in here?" I yelled. Heads turned. Finally, the attention I deserved. "This guy was trying to shove some drug down my throat." By now the guy was running out the door.

"You need to chill," the bartender said, smiling a little, but his teeth were clenched. Cute but not my type.

"You need better screening!" I said loudly, enjoying the attention. I got up on a chair, managing not to fall. "How many of you people would like a better class of customer?"

A few people raised their hands. Most others went back to talking or drinking or sulking, which was behavior I'd noticed a lot of in hipster hangouts.

The bartender wiggled the chair, and I tumbled off into

his arms. "Time to go, Debbie."

I hate that name. "I'm Deb, and I'm a paying customer!" I was grabbed by both arms from behind by Neal, the bouncer. "OK, OK, I'm leaving," I growled, leaning over to pick up my bag. I saw the little green-and-white capsule on the floor and picked it up then dropped it into my pocket. Neal, whose breath always smelled of beer (probably a job perk), led me out, to scattered applause. I turned and bowed, but no one called for an encore.

❧❧❧

The next morning, my phone buzzed annoyingly, waking me up. A text from Ethan. *Where are you?*

I was just getting back to sleep when my phone buzzed again. It was Becky, who left a voicemail: "Ethan is worried about you. Me too. Call, please."

I texted Becky: *I'm on vacation. Leave me alone.*

By Wednesday, I had another text from Ethan and a voicemail from Becky. I didn't reply. But I was annoyed, so I took a downer Ian had given me to get back to sleep.

❧❧❧

Ian found me Wednesday night, or Thursday morning, sitting on the floor, leaning against the wall outside my apartment. "I couldn't find my keys," I said. I looked up at him. "Are you OK? You're all blurry."

Ian tried my door. It was unlocked. I went inside and flopped down on my new bed with smelly sheets.

That weekend I went to more clubs: Nobody's Home,

The Glass Outhouse, and some no-name place in a basement, making new friends whose names I never could remember at each stop. "Hey, what's up?" always worked. Loud music and louder talk. I smiled, nodded, and accompanied my nameless besties to the restroom, where we snorted lines and puffed on funny-looking cigarettes.

If one of my new friends said, "Try this," I tried it. They were all just versions of pain control. I knew that if I stopped, the shrapnel or glass would start poking at my brain. I was just doing what any girl whose grandparents had been murdered and knew the real murderer had gotten away with it would do.

☙☙☙

On Sunday, I went to back to Captain Nemo. I was not 86'ed. It was crowded because of some hot new band playing, I forget their name. I looked around for a place to sit, and a guy and a girl, looking like they'd just gotten off work at an office, beckoned to me. They pointed to an empty chair at their table. I sat down.

"Hi," the girl said. "I'm Jess, this is Alan." Jess had red hair and a nice smile. Alan looked like my brother: blue eyes, dimpled chin, a lock of brown hair hanging over his forehead. We wedged onto the dance floor, rubbing body parts with strangers for a while, squeezed together like rush hour on the crosstown. The band took a break.

I ordered drinks, and Jess pulled an Altoids tin from her purse and took out a yellow pill. "It's Molly," she said. "Want to try?" I didn't know Molly from Madonna, but Jess and Alan both took one, so why not?

About two minutes later, I was in love with Jess and

Alan, all the other nameless people in the room, the band, the waitress, and Neal, the sweaty bouncer at the door. Alan, or maybe it was Jess, kissed me, and I hugged whoever it was.

The three of us went outside, and Jess hailed a cab. I passed out, waking up when they were helping me up some stairs. I loved them. Then we were in an apartment that smelled of incense and bug spray, and we all fell onto a bed that was hanging in midair. I floated away on it.

I woke up, and someone was rubbing me and kissing my neck. It felt good. Someone else was kissing me on the lips, and I kissed back, and then the world dissolved into blue and green.

I woke up in the dark sandwiched between Jess and Alan, who were both snoring. Did I have sex? I didn't think so. I still had my clothes on. I wasn't sure if that was a good thing or a bad thing. I boosted myself off the bed and tiptoed out the door.

I went downstairs and sat on the front stairs, smelling frying grease from the Chinese restaurant. Still nighttime. I closed my eyes and looked at the inside of my head. I think I passed out.

I don't know how long it was before I felt a pair of hands lifting me up. "Alan?" I asked. The hands picked me up. Alan was stronger than he looked. I was being carried somewhere. "Put me down, Alan," I said.

"Shut up, bitch."

That was not Alan. I opened my eyes, and three guys were dragging me down the block and into the alley. I fought, trying to break free, but someone punched me on the side of my head.

I was thrown down. I felt rough pavement under my

knees. I grabbed a garbage bin to pull myself up, and I saw them: a guy with a beard and a shaved head, another wearing a hoodie, the third coming toward me with a knife in his hand had long black hair and acne.

"Me first," Acne Guy said as he grabbed my arm and shoved me down to my knees. I crawled down the alley, but he yanked me back, pulling my jeans down. He leaned over and put the knife to my throat. "This'd be easier if you just gave up."

Acne Guy grabbed me by the collar and shoved my head down on a wooden crate, holding it with one hand while he pulled my underpants down with the other.

"Hurry up, Aaron!" I heard a high-pitched voice. I turned my head to see Baldy looking back down the alley. Acne guy was named Aaron. Not that it mattered.

Aaron said, "Asshole! I told you no names! Now we gotta kill her!"

"Right. Like we were gonna let her go!" A laugh that sounded like a bark from Hoodie.

"Help! Help!" I yelled, but I got my head slammed down on the crate, and a hand smelling of cigarettes went over my mouth.

I bit down on it, felt my teeth break the skin and tasted blood. Aaron screamed. "Goddamn you!" He let my head go, and I rolled to one side off the crate, stood, and pulled my jeans up. I felt blood running down my face. I started to run down the alley, but Baldy blocked my way.

"Is this fun or what?" He grinned, showing a missing front tooth.

Aaron came toward me, knife in his bloody hand. "You don't get it, sweets. It's over for you."

Aaron jabbed at me with his knife, and I ducked to one

side—and got a fist in the stomach from Baldy. I doubled over, a pain like hot oil. Aaron shoved me onto the pavement, ripping my jeans and underpants down to my knees. I felt him come at me from behind. I tried to pull away, but my legs were tangled in my pants. Baldy pushed me down, holding my shoulders.

My bleeding head was on the greasy concrete, my stomach a fireball of agony.

CHAPTER

I heard Hoodie's high-pitched voice: "Hey! Scram, asshole!"
I heard a new voice, deeper. "I think not. Let her go.
You'll be better off."

Baldy took his hands off my shoulders, and I felt Aaron move away from my bare ass. I rolled over on my back, leaned against the brick wall, and pulled up my pants. A tall man wearing a black knit cap and a blue bandana over his face, stood, legs apart, at the end of the alley. He moved forward a step, and the streetlight behind turned him into a silhouette. Hoodie pulled out a gun. Some website in my brain registered it: a .32 Beretta.

It might have been the pink pills in my bloodstream, the streetlight shining in my eyes, or maybe I just blinked. Bandana blurred for a second, I heard a crack, and Hoodie screamed. "You broke my arm! You broke my arm!" Then Hoodie was on his face on the pavement, his arm twisted to one side, Bandana holding the Beretta. In what seemed like two seconds, Bandana ejected the magazine, jacked the round from the chamber, and tossed them to the side. They clattered on the pavement.

Aaron yanked up his pants. "Now you're gonna die!" he

said, waving his knife.

Baldy grabbed a thick wooden stick off the ground, and he and Aaron stepped toward Bandana, one moving left, the other moving right, circling, moving in. Aaron jabbed his knife, but Bandana saw it coming and yanked Baldy's arm as he raised the stick to strike. I watched, but it was still a blur. It looked like Bandana pulled Baldy toward Aaron's knife, then as Aaron jerked his knife away, moved behind Aaron and kicked him in the back of his knee. Aaron grabbed his leg and fell to the pavement, groaning.

Baldy swung his stick at Bandana, and in another move too fast to see, Bandana was suddenly behind Baldy, slamming him headfirst against the brick wall. He crumpled to the asphalt.

Aaron staggered to his feet, the knife still in his hand, and lunged at Bandana, who turned sideways, pulling Aaron's knife arm towards him, throwing him off-balance. Bandana stuck out his foot, and Aaron fell. Bandana looked at him for a second then came over to me.

I put out my hands, a pathetic attempt to protect myself. He reached out his hand to me. I shoved it off. "No! Go away!"

Behind him, Aaron, who was not a quitter, got up again and came at Bandana from behind. Before I could yell, Bandana ducked and rolled backward. He grabbed Aaron's knife hand with one hand and punched Aaron right in the crotch with the other. Aaron screamed and doubled over. Bandana lept to his feet and kicked Aaron in the head. Aaron collapsed like wet paper.

Bandana came over to me, and I kicked at him. "No! No!"

He leaned down, the light from a window above showing

his amber eyes, looking like they were glowing in the dark, and I smelled peppermint. "Get away from me!" I yelled, pushing at him.

He shoved my arms aside. "Stop. I'm saving your skinny ass." Bandana picked me up and threw me over his shoulder like a sack of potatoes. I beat against his back with my fists until the pain in my head and stomach jumped on me with both feet, and I passed out.

কৈকৈকৈ

I was at the beach, at our favorite spot on the sand just down from Café Volna, where we sometimes had lunch. Grandma Nadiya, in her nineteenth-century ankle-length skirt, high-necked blouse, and straw hat, sat on one of our old wooden beach chairs, our big white and green umbrella shading her. Grandpa Viktor, at the water's edge, held little Ethan's hand. The sun was bright and warm. I ran across the hot sand to the water to cool off. Grandma called after me: "*Bud'te oberezhni, doroha.*" "Be careful, darling." The water was cold on my feet. I knew I could walk out for a long way before I was up to my waist.

I waded in, but suddenly the water was up to my neck. I got scared. I turned to look for Grandpa, but he was gone. I couldn't see our umbrella. I tried to walk back to the shore, but the sand beneath my feet was soft, and my feet were sinking into it. The water was rising—to my chin, to my nose. I opened my mouth to cry out, but water filled it. I was choking, drowning.

I tried to swim, but my arms were tangled in cloth, and then I was awake, fighting a blue blanket that covered me. I threw it off, opened my eyes, and looked around.

I woke up surrounded by green plastic curtains in a pale green room. I was in a hospital bed, wearing a blue gown, with a thing in my nose and a needle connected to a plastic tube stuck in my wrist. My head hurt, and I had a pain in my stomach. To my right, a monitor registered my vitals.

"Hello?" I called out. "Hello?"

The plastic curtains parted, and a young, brown-skinned woman in green scrubs came in. "Hello back," she said cheerfully, her smile showing white teeth. She looked at her clipboard. "Deborah. How are you feeling?" She straightened out the blankets. Her nametag had 'Lupita Monacala, New York-Presbyterian Hospital' printed on it.

"Like someone punched me and slammed my head against a wall," I said. I wasn't feeling jolly, but her cheerfulness was contagious.

"The good news is, you don't have a concussion, no broken ribs, or any internal bleeding," she said, leaning over to check my bandaged head. "The not-so-good news, your blood workup showed a lot of drugs inside you," she said, making a tsk-tsk noise.

I tried to sit up, and my stomach reminded me of what had happened in the alley. I flopped back down. "Ow. How long have I been here? How'd I get here?"

"Since about two this morning. A young man brought you here. The night shift told me he carried you over his shoulder," Lupita said, with a little chuckle. "Like a sack of masa."

It came back to me. Someone, his movements a blur, had taken out three armed men. Lupita pulled back the plastic curtains around my bed, and there were Ethan and Becky. "Visitors."

I tried a smile, but my face hurt. "Hi." I fumbled around for the button to raise the bed. Lupita bent down and did it for me.

"What the hell, Deb!" Ethan started, but Becky punched him hard in the shoulder. Ethan rubbed his arm. "Ow."

Becky came to the bedside, leaned over, and kissed me. "I'm so glad—" she looked over her shoulder—"we're so glad you're all right. Quite a vacation, huh?" She grinned.

Ethan took my hand. "We hadn't heard from you. This morning, the hospital called…"

I smiled back at him. He was trying to be nice, a good brother. "Yeah. Sorry about that. I got in over my head," I said.

Becky took Ethan's arm and turned to go. Over her shoulder, she said, "Get dressed. We'll take you home."

Lupita showed me the little closet where my stuff was, and I got up, feeling stiff and creaky. I got dressed, signed some papers, filled the prescription Lupita had given me with a frosty look. "Take just one or two when you absolutely need to, for the pain, not to get high. Don't do that no more," she told me.

At the entrance, we passed a woman wearing a nametag on a ribbon around her neck, New York Children's Services. She had her arm around a scared, teary-eyed little girl of maybe ten. Two NYPD cops in uniform were hovering near-by, and I overheard snatches of their conversation: "…She ran away…" "…Three other kids in a basement somewhere…"

Ethan parked Becky's silver BMW in front of my apartment building, which looked even more rundown in daylight. I said no thanks to Becky's offer to help me upstairs. I didn't want her or Ethan to see how I lived. I needed something for the pain, so I took four of the prescription pills, had one of Ian's magic joints, and fell onto the bed, the smell of rotting food fading away. If I had any dreams, I didn't remember them.

෨෨෨

I heard a noise in my apartment. My eyelids had glue on them. A blast of white light shone through. Someone had opened the curtains.

"Get up," someone said.

"Go away," I replied, my voice sounding like it was filtered through rusty tin cans and wet plaster. Was it a robber? Maybe. I tried to get up, but my legs wouldn't move. I managed to peel open one eye, but the light hurt too much. Someone grabbed my shoulders and shook them.

"Stop it," I said, rolling away. My face hit something, and I opened one eye again, noticing I was on the floor next to my bed.

Becky was kneeling over me. "Get up. Get up."

I tried to push her arms away, but she was stronger than she looked or than I was. "All right, all right!" Becky moved back and I sat up. I rubbed my eyes, managing to open both of them at once. "You just dropped me off. What are you doing here?"

"That was yesterday," Becky said. She wrinkled her nose. "It stinks in here. Like garbage."

Like something died, I thought. I sat on my bed, which also stank. Maybe that's why I wound up on the floor.

Becky walked the five steps to the kitchen sink and started washing dishes. "You have cockroaches," she said over her shoulder.

"Along with everyone else in the East Village," I replied. "How'd you get in?"

"Your friend Ian." Becky picked up a dish, then dropped it in the sink. "Ugh! It looks like you're breeding them."

I snorted. "Very funny. Not."

"Ethan thought that you wanted to be left alone. But I decided you did not." Becky wiped her hands on her pants after picking up and dropping a brownish dish towel. She sat down beside me, holding up the bottle of painkillers from the floor. "What are you doing?" she asked.

I looked down at the floor. "Having fun." A wise-ass answer.

Becky lifted me to my feet and dragged me into the bathroom, about four steps. She held my head, forcing me to look in the mirror. "Is this the face of someone having fun?"

A girl I didn't know looked back at me. Her blonde hair was a tangled mess, she had a giant bruise on the side of her head and a scabbed-over scratch on her cheek. Her eyes' blue pupils were wrapped in a roadmap of red highways and byways. And she smelled bad. Fun. Yeah. A fun victim.

"Let go." I pulled away from Becky and went to flop back on the bed. "Leave me alone."

Becky sat on the bed. "Why are you doing this to yourself?"

I turned away, looking out the grimy window. "I told you. I'm having fun." I pointed to the door. "And you can leave now. You're no fun."

"If Ethan knew you were doing this to yourself—"

"Tell him! I don't give a shit! Invite him over! We'll do Jell-O shots!" I sat up in bed, glaring at this annoying woman who'd invaded my space. "Now get the hell out."

Becky got up and went to the sink. "Do you have a clean glass? I want a drink of water."

"Look around."

Becky took a glass from the counter, stared at it for a second, then washed it and filled it. She came over and hurled the water in my face. I raised my hand to hit her, then stopped. Water ran down my cheeks, and then water started coming from my eyes. I wiped them away, but the tears kept coming. All of them. From that night when I came to see my grandparents carried out on gurneys, from the funeral, from every time I pushed the tears away. I sat down on the bed, my face in my hands, sobbing. Becky sat next to me, her arm around my shoulders.

"Every time you come over, we fight and you make me cry," I said.

"No. I help you find the tears inside you," Becky replied, and I noticed that tears were on her cheeks.

Becky handed me a slightly grimy towel, or maybe it was a t-shirt. I wiped my eyes and blew my nose. Something like shame, maybe, made me blush. "Sorry," I said. We stood up together and clung tightly to each other for a moment, medium-sized white girl and tall black girl.

Becky grabbed my shoulders and pointed me to the bathroom. "Go wash your face."

When I came out, Becky was putting bedding, towels, clothes, and things on top of a sheet. She pulled up the corners and tied them together. A breeze came in through one of the two windows she'd propped open. I put on sort of clean jeans and a t-shirt that passed the smell test.

Becky shoved some dirty clothes off my chair and sat, looking up at me and making me uncomfortable. Time for the "say no to drugs" lecture.

"Tell me why you did this," she said, waving her arm to include robbing my college fund, my phony ID, my drugs, my apartment, the street, New York, the world. Not the lecture.

I told Becky. I told her about the phone hang-ups and the search of my house. I found my Coach bag under the bed, took out the photo of her and Ethan, Dobby's dried blood still on it, and showed it to her. "If I'd kept on doing what I was doing..."

Becky took a deep breath and nodded. "You are hiding. To protect me and Ethan."

"Whoever it was, he made his point. You'd be in danger. I had something he wanted, and maybe he thinks I know something. Which I don't." Tears stung the corners of my eyes again, and I wiped them away.

"You should have told me," Becky said.

I stood up, angry again. Maybe at Becky, more likely at myself. "Yeah, right!" I started pacing the floor, about six steps in any direction. "You'd have wanted me to keep on going, you'd have pushed me and pushed me, and I couldn't...I can't..." I flopped down on the floor, cross-legged, looking up at her. "You're a warrior. I'm not."

Becky reached down and pulled me to my feet. "No, you're not." Her brown eyes looked into my blue ones for a long few seconds. "Your grandfather knew. You are a she-wolf." She bent down and reached behind me, pulling something out from under the pile of dirty laundry: the she-wolf picture, with a smudged black Louboutin boot print on the white matte. "I found this under the bed."

Shit. Shit.

Becky put the picture in the big bag she always carried. "I know where we can get this re-matted. Are you hungry?"

❧❧❧

We went to Anderson's Fine Art on lower Broadway, where tweedy and bespectacled Mr. Anderson said he'd have the picture in a new matte tomorrow. Then we went to lunch at a diner on the corner. I hadn't had a regular meal in a while.

"It seems to me," Becky said, pointing at me with her fork, "that if someone thinks you know something, you should find out what that is."

"How? All I've got is Grandpa's ledger with a bunch of code words, things written in some dead language!" I wished I hadn't used that word. Sharp things poked around inside my head.

Becky took out her phone and scrolled through photos to the image of Father Andy's translation. "Did you look up the Bible chapters?"

"No. But I don't even know if they are from the Bible." Guilt washed over me like the scummy waters of the Salt Marsh, shoving and pushing the sharp things. We finished our meal in silence.

We paid and left. Outside on the sidewalk, Becky gave me a quick hug. "When you decide to do something, call me. I will make sure that Ethan and I are safe. We can go away. Don't worry about us. Do your laundry."

CHAPTER 14

I watched the dryer spin for a while. On the empty plastic chair next to me was yesterday's *New York Post*. I flipped through the pages. On page six was a photo of three guys: Aaron, Baldy, and Hoodie, my almost rapist-killers. They were surrounded by cops, their faces swollen and puffy. Aaron's greasy hair hung beneath his bandaged head and fell over two black eyes; his arm was in a sling. Hoodie's arm was in a cast. Baldy was lying on a gurney, his head wrapped in bandages. The headline said: "Thugs Delivered to 7th Precinct."

I gathered up my now clean stuff and left the laundromat. Around the corner from my apartment, a pale girl who looked younger than me, all hunched over in a filthy sweatshirt and torn jeans, was squatting on a plastic box on the corner of Mott. She stared down at the sidewalk, coiling her stringy blonde hair in her fingers and humming some tuneless song. She looked familiar, maybe someone I'd known in school.

"Hi," I said.

She jumped. "What do you want?" she asked in a croak.

"Nothing. Just saying hi."

"You got any fentanyl, oxy?" She looked up at me with red-rimmed eyes.

"No. But I've got a granola bar." I took a bar from my shirt pocket and held it out to her.

She shoved my hand away. "You got any money?" She held out her hand, her sleeve sliding up to show tiny reddish-brown needle marks on her pale white arm.

"I'll be back. Don't go away." I walked up the street to the bodega on the corner and bought some fruit, a carton of milk, and some energy bars. I came back and handed her the bag. "Eat something. Don't kill yourself. I've tried it. It's no fun," I said. She took the bag, peered into it, put it on the sidewalk and resumed twisting her hair.

In my apartment, I went to the bathroom, turned on the shower, stripped, and looked in the mirror. A butterfly bandage on my temple, a swollen lower lip, a fist-sized blue bruise on my stomach, my stylish bob a matted mess. I knew why that girl on the corner looked familiar. I stood there as steam from the shower coated the mirror until I couldn't see myself.

જ્ઞ જ્ઞ જ્ઞ

My dreams had been gathering, waiting in line for a drug-free sleep. I spent the night jogging along the fence, the mysterious other person keeping pace, running on the beach, chasing someone who'd vanish when I'd get close. Running. Running. Running.

I was in a dark place, but I could hear Grandpa's voice reassuring me: *How many rounds, zaichik?*

I thought, *Seven rounds, Didus.*

How accurate?

Up to fifty feet.

A chuckle. *Only if you are very, very good. And if there is no wind, if you are not in a hurry, under stress, or distracted.*

Twenty-five feet.

Or less. What are some problems?

Hammer out of alignment, poorly made hand loads, single action takes time.

かかか

The next day, after I picked up the she-wolf picture from Anderson, I spent a couple of hours walking around the neighborhood trying to find my rescuer. "Tall guy, wears a stocking cap and a blue bandanna over his face?" Shaking of heads, shrugs.

An old white-haired waiter at the Ukrainian restaurant helped. When he brought my sandwich and Pellegrino, I asked him. He straightened his stooped back and smiled. "Ustym," he said.

"What's an Ustym?" I asked. He put my plate on the table and looked around to see if anyone was listening. Then he told me the restaurant's owner had been paying protection to some gang until the gang leader was found in an alley, beaten almost to death, arms and legs broken. A dealer selling drugs to fifth graders outside schools had disappeared. A street person looking for a meal in a trash bin found two creeps who'd been doing home invasions inside it, tied up and beaten bloody.

"Do you know how I can find him?" I asked.

The waiter shook his head. "No one does."

৯৯৯

I started to run again. At first, I just jogged around my neighborhood, able to do a mile or two before pooping out. It was all about getting into shape, I kept telling myself. That's it. But something was going on, despite whatever I told myself.

While I ran, I started noticing guys in stocking caps; I counted fifteen in a week. The sharp, black metallic things in my head were still there. I hadn't drowned them in alcohol or dulled them with drugs. Maybe they never went away, but they were benign tumors, something I might learn to live with. Maybe they were poking me to do something.

I started going to a gym on Mulberry Street. Most mornings it was packed with high-tech machines; sweaty, testosterone-fueled guys; and stringy-muscled women. I felt out of place, but decided to focus on myself: weights, treadmill, leg machines. After a week, I began to get back to my twelfth-grade cross-country shape.

One day I saw a huge bodybuilder guy working out with the big bag. His fists hit the bag with satisfying thumps. He looked over at me and nodded, not smiling.

Almost without my noticing, my arms started twitching, and I'd curled my fingers into fists. The big guy stopped the bag from swinging, turned to me, and gestured to it.

I took two swings at the bag. My hands felt like I'd punched a concrete wall. I kept jabbing at the bag, which totally ignored me. After five minutes, my arms hurt, my shoulders felt like they were coming out of their sockets, and my knuckles were bleeding. I went into the locker room and ran my hands under the cold water. Enough for now. I decided to come back later to finish my workout. I went back to my apartment and showered, letting the hot water heal my aching shoulders. I dried myself, dressed, and squirted Bactine on my knuckles.

I went back to the gym that evening. As I came in, someone held the front door to let me pass. I nodded, then looked again. He was twentysomething, tall, thin, with amber eyes and wearing a black knit cap on his blonde head.

I turned, touching his arm. "You're him," I said. "Ustym."

Something flickered across his face but was gone in an instant. "My name is Ozzie." He was out the door before I could react.

I rushed outside and put my hand on his back. "Wait." I took a deep breath. "I'm Deborah. Thank you."

"Forget it. I always hold the door."

"It was you. In the alley. You saved me from those creeps," I said.

Ozzie shook his head. "Not me. Must have been somebody else." He turned and walked away.

I ran to catch up with him and blocked his path. He started to step around me, looking annoyed. He slung his gym bag over his shoulder. "Go bother somebody else. I've got things to do."

I leaned forward, smelled his breath. Peppermint. He pushed me away and walked down the street. Again, I caught up to him. "What you did—how you fought those guys. I want to learn that. I want to learn how to fight."

"The gym has classes. Sign up."

"I'll pay you."

He turned back to me, laughing, more of a sneer. "Buy your way into a pile of shit, buy your way out. Typical."

"Screw you. You don't know anything about me."

"There are a hundred just like you in this neighborhood," Ozzie replied. "Lost girls looking for something to drown their so-called pain in whatever poison they can shoot, snort, drink, or smoke. Little Cassie on the corner. She'll be dead before she's sixteen."

The girl who'd asked me for drugs, I guessed.

Ozzie walked away, saying over his shoulder, "Leave me alone. Go take a class."

I watched him go, angry at him for being a jerk and for maybe being right. He turned the corner, and I ran to catch him, but he'd disappeared in the crowd coming out of a movie on Broadway.

I started going to the gym at night. But amber-eyed, peppermint-flavored Ozzie was never there. I thought for a minute or so that I'd scared him away. Then I laughed at my suddenly inflated self. Laughing at myself. That's something.

పాపాపా

I changed my routine, working out in the mornings, the afternoons, and evenings on different days. When I went running in the neighborhood, I made a point of stopping for coffee at the place across the street from the gym, sitting in a table by the window, watching. I felt like a stalker. And I was.

It took a week before I saw him again while he was entering the gym. I ran across Mulberry Street, catching up to him as he waved his pass at the card reader on the front desk.

"Teach me how to fight," I said.

"You again?" He turned away and headed for the locker room.

I ran past him to the door, blocking his way. "I need to

know how to do what you do," I said. I remembered asking Grandpa again and again to teach me.

"I told you. Take a class." He pointed to a list on a corkboard next to the door. "See? 'Beginning self-defense.' Monday, Wednesday, Friday." Ozzie stepped around me and entered the locker room.

I was angry—at him for being a stubborn as I was, at myself for…I wasn't sure what. Those sharp things in my head were stirring around, though.

After a few days on the big bag, my knuckles got tougher. Once in a while I saw Ozzie and asked him to teach me how to fight, but he kept saying, "Take a class."

I left notes in his gym bag: *Teach me.* One night I went to the gym around midnight to wait for him. He came out, and I followed him to an apartment building on Broome, across from the Holy Trinity church. I stood by the door until someone came out of the building, walked in, and stuck a note in his mailbox: *Teach me.*

One evening, I was punching the big bag, thinking I might make it move three inches today, when I felt someone looking at me. It was Ozzie, wearing sweatpants and a sleeveless shirt. I stopped and went over to him.

"Teach me."

"You don't give up, do you?"

Actually, I do. I'd given up trying to get better grades than Ethan, given up trying to run faster than Brianna. I'd given up finding my grandparents' killer. I'd almost given up my life. "Please," I said. "It's important."

He rolled his amber eyes. "OK. Tomorrow, here, eight o'clock. If you're late, we're done. If you whine, we're done. If you ask too many questions, we're done."

"Eight a.m. or eight p.m.? Or does that count as a question?"

Ozzie almost smiled. "Morning," he said. "Give me your phone."

I handed it to him, and he punched in a number then handed it back. He walked to the locker room. He turned at the door. "Don't think you're going to be punching anything for a while."

ॐ ॐ ॐ

We started the next day. Ozzie pointed to a pullup bar. "Put your left leg on the bar."

No problem, I thought. I'd been running, doing stretches. I was pretty limber. I kicked up, put my ankle over the bar, and fell down.

"Again," he said. Again, I fell down.

That first week, Ozzie's training was all about balance and speed. If you're going to kick someone in the head, you have to be able to swing your leg up there, not just once but twice, three times. I worked out with Ozzie at the gym every day for two hours. I thought I'd been working out before, but this was nothing like the wimpy stuff I was doing. I came back to my apartment at the end of our sessions and collapsed.

The second week, we went to my enemy, the big bag. "You need to learn how to hit like a girl. I mean, really hit like a girl. You hit like a baby," Ozzie said.

I learned how to move the big bag, using my fists and my feet. Ozzie taught a fighting style I'd never heard of, Krav Maga. "In street fighting, there's one rule: There are no rules.

If someone wants to hurt you, your only choices are to let them or to hurt them enough so they stop."

Ozzie showed me how to punch five times more quickly than I could punch once. I remembered the blur of his arms from that night in the alley. He taught me the body's weak points: the eyes, the throat, the groin, the knees. I learned my strong points: my knee, my elbow, the heel of my hand. I learned how to disable an attacker by striking upward at the nose and by making a V with my thumb and fingers to hit the throat. I struggled to overcome my tendency to step back from someone with a club, a knife, or a gun. I stepped to them so I could push the weapon, twist the arm, knee 'em in the balls.

Ozzie turned his back to me. "Put your arm around my throat. Choke me." I swung my arm around his neck from behind and grabbed my wrist with my other hand. He reached up and pinched under my upper arm. The pain was so bad I screamed, causing a few gym rats to turn and look.

Ozzie pointed to the back of his thigh. "There's a nerve like that in your upper leg too. Pinch hard."

I stepped to his side and pinched his leg as hard as I could where he'd showed me. He just laughed. "Get a pair of hand exercisers."

I bought the heavy-duty pair of Grip Masters at Modell's. It took three days before I could squeeze them more than once.

We worked out with punch mitts on his hands so I could practice hitting. Day after day, I got stronger—not just my arms, but my shoulders and my whole body. Ozzie smiled, taking off his mitts. "You make my hands hurt, Deborah."

Getting all obsessive, like I'd done with cross-country

and guns, I watched dozens of YouTube street fighting and Krav Maga videos. A link led me to a fighting style called Wing Chun, and I practiced for hours. I showed Ozzie a couple of moves, and he nodded. "It's all good. It's about what works for you."

I learned how to find my balance, to take a punch, to roll back and let my attacker come to me, off-balance. After a couple of weeks, I had bruises, aches, and pains in places I'd never had them before. I also had muscles in some of the same places.

At first it was just practicing, learning something new. I'd made myself a victim, and the attack in the alley proved it. I decided that if I was going to die, it'd be on my own terms— barring getting run over by a bus or struck by lightning or something. But the more I practiced, the more something in me took over. In my mind I attacked the killer of my grandparents, I shattered his nose, I crushed his windpipe, I transformed his face into a bloody pulp of skin and sinew, something left on the floor of a slaughterhouse.

One day, Ozzie grabbed my arm. "Stop. Stop."

"Am I doing it wrong?"

"You're letting your emotions take over. They are eating you up from the inside. They get in the way of your skills. Step back."

I didn't know what he meant. Well, maybe I did. But I felt I was a little bit more in charge of myself.

∽∽∽

One afternoon, Ozzie threw me to the mat, and I aimed a kick at his stomach, which he easily deflected. But I'd learned. I whipped my other leg when he was off-balance and tripped him. He fell across from me, and I rolled to my feet and came down on him astride his chest, pinning his arms with my knees.

"That's almost good," Ozzie smiled up at me. "But you want your attacker face down on the ground."

"I know," I said. Then I leaned down and kissed him. For a long moment, he kissed me back. I tasted the sweat on his lip mingling with mine, peppermint and shaving cream. Suddenly he threw me off him, and I tumbled onto my side onto the mat, surprised. "What?"

Ozzie got up and without a word went into the locker room. I worked out on the big bag, which was near the men's locker room, for half an hour, but Ozzie didn't show. Finally, I took a deep breath, went to the locker room door, and yelled, "Hello?" No one answered, so I went in. Against the yellow tile back wall was a door marked Exit.

I went back to my apartment, showered and changed, then texted him. I left a message: "I'm sorry. I made a mistake." I walked over to his apartment on Broome, but no one answered the door. One day, I saw his gray-haired Ukrainian landlady, sweeping the steps. "No, my dear, I have not seen Ustym."

The day after that and the day after that, I went to the gym at my regular time, but Ozzie was not there. The next day and the next, I went to his apartment, but he wasn't there. I called but got voicemail. I worked out on the big bag, swinging it back and forth, putting my own face on it, hitting it harder and harder until tears came.

I went shopping for groceries at the Whole Foods on Houston and found a jar of borscht. I put it in one of my brand-new pans and warmed it up. The smell—beets and cabbage—hurled me back to the kitchen on Second Street. Before I knew it, the soup was boiling over, and I was crying.

CHAPTER 15

That Saturday, the Q train wasn't crowded. The long trip under the river ended when the cars rattled above ground. A little bit of morning sun was peeking through the clouds. The house, my home, looked just like it always had when I came home from school.

Hi, Grandma. I'm home.

So? How was school? What have you learned, vnuchka?

Let's see. I learned to stop being a victim. To stop covering pain with drugs. How to defend myself. Not to kiss my trainer.

I parked the suitcase at the door and looked through the pile of mail on the entry hall table that Mrs. Krasny had kindly sorted for me. Bills, ads, and a dozen squarish fancy paper envelopes that probably held condolence cards. I tossed the cards and the ads in the trash. I took the bills into Grandpa's office where he paid them, writing the checks in his spidery hand.

More bills. Always more bills.

I heard Grandma and Grandpa in my head and it wasn't torture anymore, not the shrapnel their voices had been.

I bounced the suitcase up the stairs to my room, put my fancy underwear and designer tops into drawers, and tossed a bunch of my old clothes in a corner for Goodwill or recycling. I hung Becky's wolf picture on the wall so I could see it from my bed. I opened some windows to let the stale air out then went running.

☙☙☙

I was heading back home, cooling off while walking down Ocean, when I saw a line of cars and a dozen people in front of a funeral home. No more funerals, I thought, starting to cross the street. But when I got closer, I saw that it wasn't a Ukrainian crowd; I recognized Graciela Montez, a Puerto Rican girl I knew from high school. A dozen others, mostly Puerto Rican, stood on the sidewalk. I walked past a police car; in it, a cop was drinking coffee.

In my Nikes, running shorts, and Ethan's Princeton sweatshirt, I wasn't dressed for the event. I found my way to the back of the line of Puerto Rican folks and tugged on Graciela's black blouse.

She turned and her jaw dropped. "Jesus, Deb." She put her hand on my shoulder. "Sorry about your grandparents."

"Thanks," I said.

"What happened to you? Where've you been?"

"Kind of a vacation. Whose funeral?"

Graciela wiped a tear from her eye. "Maria Sanchez. CC's mom."

We had met in seventh grade. CC was Carlos, who wanted everyone to call him Charlie. We compromised on Carlos-Charlie, or CC. We had a couple of classes together. His mom was nice. She made us black beans and rice and fried plantains when I went over for dinner. In the eighth grade, CC and I were kind of boyfriend-girlfriend. We went to the movies, necked a few times, and I let him squeeze my boobs in the park. Afterward I went to Millennium, he went to Brooklyn High, and that was the end of our teen romance.

Graciela whispered, as others in the crowd began to glare at us, "She was murdered."

It came back in a rush: my house, burned siding above the broken bay window. Police cars and fire trucks blocking the street. Yellow tape across the white picket fence. The smell of smoke. White-coated men wheeling two gurneys holding body bags to a black van. Grandma's flowers trampled. Me screaming and crying. Large tattooed arms wrapped around me, holding me back.

After a moment, I asked "Where's CC?"

Graciela looked around nervously. She nodded her head at the funeral home. She whispered, "Inside. He's hiding." She wiped her eyes again. "He told me his mom's killer is after him." She made an angry face. "He can't even go to the cemetery."

The black hearse with silver trim pulled up to the curb in front of the funeral home. The crowd in front of the door parted to let pass four men carrying a brown wooden casket with brass handles. Some older women wearing black dresses and scarves wiped their eyes.

I wanted to find CC. I went into the alley next to the funeral home. There was a door halfway down. Of course it was locked. I pounded on it until a very thin Black dude in a black suit and with a little goatee opened it. He looked annoyed. "The entrance is—"

"I know. But I didn't want to bother anyone at such a

sad time." I smiled in what I hoped was a sympathetic way. "I came in with my cousin yesterday to look at caskets, and I think I left my cell in the ladies' room." I was getting better at spur of the moment lying.

The dude let me in. We walked down the sconce-lit hallway, and he glanced sideways at me, trying to remember if he'd seen me yesterday. I hoped I'd find CC before he figured out I hadn't been there. I went into the ladies' room in the wood-paneled hallway. I heard a man's voice say, "Eugene, we need you in front." I peered out the door to see Eugene hurrying away. There was a sign over a door at the other end of the hall: Chapel.

It was dim inside and smelled of candle wax. Organ music was playing over speakers. Sunlight glowed through a stained-glass window. Someone in a suit that was too big for him was sitting in one of the padded chairs, his head down.

It took me a second to recognize my middle school sweetie. His face was thin, with a wispy beard. His black hair was uncombed. He leapt up, frightened, then saw it was me.

"Hey," I said, then put my arms around him.

CC stiffened, then relaxed. I felt his chest heave with a sob he tried to swallow. "Deb…"

"I'm so sorry about your mom."

We sat down. CC told me he'd been dealing drugs in the neighborhood for a big-time dealer named Two-Ray. One night two weeks ago CC had gotten jumped, and the muggers had taken his stash and about two thousand bucks.

Two-Ray had a reputation on the street for torturing and killing dealers who'd stolen from him, and there was no reason to think he'd believe the story. CC went into hiding. But he didn't know just how vicious Two-Ray was. He and his thugs had gone to CC's apartment looking for him and killed his mother when she wouldn't give up her son.

"*Mi madre* didn't even know where I was!" CC sobbed. "I got nowhere to go. He's gonna kill me."

I blurted out, "You can stay with me."

CC shook his head. "No. You'll be in danger too."

"Listen. You know who my family is. I live in the safest house in the safest neighborhood in Brooklyn. No gangster would dare set foot on my block." *Except for the one who killed my grandparents*, I thought. *And Dobbie.*

CC wiped his eyes and looked at me. "You would do this?"

I stood up and took his hand. "Sure. But no necking, and no feeling me up."

CC smiled for a half-second. "But they've been looking for me. They know about the funeral."

"They'll think you've gone to the cemetery. Anyway, there's another exit. Come on."

As we came into the hallway, I heard cars pulling away from the front. Now was the time.

I opened the side door and peered out. Nobody in the alley. I gave CC my Princeton sweatshirt, and he put it on, pulling up the hood.

We walked up to the avenue. The last of the funeral procession was pulling away. We turned to the right, heading toward Second Street, to what used to be my home and was now maybe a refuge for CC.

Before I knew it, a cherry-red SUV with tinted windows pulled up beside us. The door swung open, and a Black guy with dreadlocks, a Jamaican flag hat, and red Converse high-tops stepped out, pointing a gun—a Beretta M9—at us.

CC started to run, but the guy said, "Don't be stupid." CC stopped and turned, a sad shrug. The guy waved the gun at me. "Stay out of the way." He grabbed CC by the sleeve and yanked him over to the car, threw him into the back seat, and got in next to him. The Escalade peeled off.

New York license RSTAMAN. I ran back to the cop car a half-block away and banged on the window. The cop was just starting up the car.

"Hey! Hey!"

He rolled down the window, looking annoyed. He had a unibrow and doughnut crumbs in his moustache. "What?"

"Didn't you see that? My friend just got grabbed by thugs and taken away!"

"It was a funeral, kid. Lotsa people getting into cars."

"Not with guns pointing at them, you—" I stopped before I called him a rude name. "Uh, officer. I got the license plate. A red SUV, maybe a Caddy—"

"Go down to the station and make a report." He put the car in gear.

I ran around to the front and blocked him, banging my hands on the hood. "Take me there!" I ran to the passenger side, opened the door, and got in.

He glared at me like I'd asked him to do something really hard, like get off his ass.

"Come on, let's go!"

"Get out of the car!"

I said the magic words. "My name is Deborah Sokolov," I read his name tag. "Officer Krupke. You know my family, I think." His expression changed from pissed off to recognition. Without a word, he started the car and drove me to the familiar 60th Precinct police station.

"I want to report a kidnapping."

Without looking up, the cop at the desk pushed a button. He pointed to a bank of ratty green chairs next to the wall. "Go sit over there. Someone will be in to see you."

Five minutes went by. Ten minutes. Then twenty. "Is today a cop holiday?" I yelled at the sergeant. He turned the page of his newspaper.

Two men in civilian clothes came through a door to my right, talking. At last, I thought, but they walked on by without looking at me. I got up and ran through the door that was closing behind them. The sergeant, reading about the real housewives of Coney Island, didn't even notice.

I was in the familiar dingy hallway that smelled of coffee and stale pizza, with windows on the left into the big room where I'd been to see O'Malley. The door I'd just come through opened, and Boris came into the hallway. He looked worried.

"Jesus, Deb, I thought you'd moved."

"I went away for a while. But I'm back. My friend CC— Carlos Sanchez—was grabbed off the street, I think by drug dealers. I got the license plate. Carlos is in real danger. Can you do something?"

Boris opened the door to the cop room, and we went in. He sat me down at an empty desk and wrote up my story on a form. "I promise you, Deborah, we'll get on this. I will see to it personally. I'll take you home."

Boris dropped me off in front of the house on Second street. I waved as he drove off, then went inside and made a sandwich. About half an hour later, my phone rang.

"Deb. It's Boris. I sent that license plate upstairs. No match."

It took me a second. "What's that mean? The plate was a fake?"

"I don't know. I gave the number to detectives. They'll ask around the neighborhood, see if there were any other witnesses." He sounded tired—and something else.

"What's going on, Boris?"

Silence. Then, whispering, he said, "It's like, like nobody's interested."

He could have been quoting O'Malley. "I know a few shop owners on the street. I'll check with them after my shift and—"

I pushed End Call. It was happening again. No one gave a crap. I was used to it. But maybe I could help CC.

I called Becky and got her voicemail. I called Ethan.

"I was wondering when you'd call," he said, by the sound of his voice still a little pissed off.

"Yeah, I know. I've been a bad little sister. But I'm home. And drug free." Pause. "Is Becky around? I need her help on something."

"Becky's out shopping. What do you need?" Ethan cleared his throat to announce that he was about to say something he didn't want to say. "Is this still about Grandma and Grandpa?"

"No. It's not about them." That was the truth. "I'm done with that." That was a lie. And I had another one. "A friend got his car dinged in the C-Town parking lot, and he wants to contact the other guy. You have to fill out a form for the DMV, and my friend just wants to, you know, keep insurance out of it. I thought Becky could use her mad skills to find the owner." I told Ethan the license plate number.

"Got it. I'll ask her when she comes back." He hung up.

Ten minutes later, I got a text from Ethan: the car, a red Escalade, was registered to a Raymond Johnson, Ozone Park. That had to be Two-Ray. I wondered how come the cops couldn't find this out. It had been hours since CC had been taken. I couldn't help him. He was probably already dead.

I went upstairs, showered, and dressed, then flopped down on my bed. The she-wolf on the wall stared at me. I turned away, but it was still there. Sharp things in my head started poking me. Maybe they weren't reminders of sadness, of helplessness. They were markers of anger that I'd almost successfully tucked away.

I'd go find CC, alive or not, and call the cops. I could at least do that much.

I got into the old Buick in our driveway. The smell of Grandpa's cigars was gone. The battery was on its last volts, but I managed to get it running.

ᪧᪧᪧ

It was dark by the time I got to Ozone Park. I parked around the corner from a one-story yellow brick industrial building on 102nd Street. The windows were boarded up, and the pull-down door was padlocked. I didn't try the front door.

I hopped a low gate on one side and went around to the back. A tiny fraction of light shone from a nearby window, and I went over to see what I could see.

Inside, dim fixtures lit a cluttered garage. The cherry-red Escalade was parked in one corner.

I heard a foot scrape the concrete behind me and turned

to see the guy wearing the red Converse high tops. He pointed his Beretta at my face. "You in the wrong place, girlie."

Ozzie lesson ten: I took a step toward him, which threw him off-guard. I spun inside his gun arm, grabbed his hand, twisting the gun away from him, and elbowing him in the face.

"Dammit, bitch!" He backed up, holding his bleeding nose. I grabbed his head with my left hand and shoved it down as I raised my knee. He dropped to his knees. "Shit!"

I pointed the Beretta at him. "Where's Carlos?"

He looked up and raised his hands, grinning a gold-toothed grin. It took me a second too long to realize why he was smiling. Something clubbed me in the back of the head, and I fell, scraping my arm on the pavement and passing out.

ஐஐஐ

My head hurt like hell. I'd forgotten Ozzie's eleventh commandment: when one person attacks, assume there's a second attacker.

I was in a small basement room lit with a single bulb hanging from the low ceiling. Dirty windows high up in the wall on one side, let in streetlights. Piles of rags, an old table with two folding chairs, and pieces of junk filled the space. I tried to move, but my arms were tied to a metal post behind me with what felt like a rope. I heard a moan from a pile of rags in one corner. It was CC. His face was bloody and swollen. He opened one eye.

"Deb?" His voice was full of pain.

"Hey. I'm here to rescue you."

CC tried to laugh, but it came out as a grunt instead. He closed his eyes. I think he passed out.

I tried pulling my hands through the ropes, but they were too tight. All I got was scraped wrists. I turned my head as far as I could to look around. In a corner to my right, a splintered wooden pallet leaned against the brick wall. Something small and shiny lay on the floor in front of it.

I scooched around on my butt to get a better look. It was a big nail, probably from the broken pallet. I stretched out my legs to try and hook it with the heel of my boot.

No luck. Just inches short. I slid further down the metal pole, walking my legs forward, bending my arms and cranking my shoulders into contortions. My knuckles pressed down on the gritty concrete behind me.

Ha. I snagged the nail with my right foot's Louboutin heel. I dragged the nail closer to me over the floor, sliding back up the pole to get it in reach. When I'd gotten it as close to my butt as I could, I scooched back around the pole so the nail was behind me, then slid down the pole so my fingers touched the floor. Stretching my hands and scraping my wrists on the rope, I could just feel it with the tip of one finger. I strained and got two fingers on it, took hold of it, and started jabbing at the ropes around my wrists.

After about five minutes, I realized this only works in movies. All I could do was poke holes through the rope fibers.

I heard heavy footsteps coming downstairs and clenched my fist to hide the nail. The door opened, and a huge Black man came in. He had to turn sideways to squeeze through the doorway. He was at least six-five, maybe three hundred pounds, and no fat. This had to be Two-Ray, as big as two ordinary Rays. Behind him entered Converse High Tops and another smaller guy, in a Knicks jersey and baggy camo shorts, probably the one who'd bashed me.

Two-Ray came over to me, grabbed me, and yanked me up with one hand to stand on my feet. The skin on my wrists scraped against the rough pole.

"You poked your head in the wrong hole," he said in a voice like diesel exhaust. "Come lookin' for your sweetie a big mistake," he nodded his basketball-sized head at CC, "unless you got the money he owe me."

Another thing that's cool in movies but not in real life is smart-ass remarks. "Will you take a check?" He slugged me with a fist as big as a canned ham. I tasted blood in my mouth.

He pulled a six-inch knife from a sheath on his belt, and I thought this was it. He reached behind me and cut the ropes. I fell to the floor, and he laughed.

"This bitty thing took your piece from you, Duane?"

Duane opened his mouth, closed it. He stammered, "She—I musta looked away—"

The other guy giggled. "You a pussy, Duane."

Duane pointed his finger at him. "Shut up, Wayne!"

"Both of you, go check the 'hood," Two-Ray said. "Keep an eye out. Make sure nobody else be waiting for her."

Wayne nodded. "Sure thing, Two-Ray. I want to do her before we kill her."

Duane nodded. "Yeah, yeah. Me too. After you, a'ight?"

"Yeah, yeah. Now go." Duane and Wayne went out the door. Two-Ray took my wallet from my bag. "Sokolov," he said, reading my real license, pronouncing it like "sookalove." "Russian? Ukrainian?"

"Yep."

Two-Ray raised his hand as if to hit me then lowered it. "You here about them drugs? Stealin' my goods?"

A good time for another lie. "I was sent to check up on you."

Two-Ray picked me up by the neck with one hand, and I struggled to breathe. "Who told you where I was? One of them cops?"

Two-Ray realized I couldn't answer with my throat being squeezed, so he threw me on my back on the wooden table. He leaned over me, holding the knife to my throat. "Tell me and I kill you quick. Or maybe I do you while I choke you out, like I did Carlos' momma." He ran his hand over my tits, down my leg, into my crotch. "She was old. But yeah, you a sweet piece."

He stuck his knife in the sheath then put his huge hand on my chest to hold me down while he started unbuttoning my jeans. I jammed the nail into his hand, and he yanked it away, dripping blood. "You're dead! You're dead!" he yelled.

He reached behind him with his other hand and pulled out a pistol, a Glock 19. I raised both my legs and kicked him as hard as I could. He staggered back maybe two inches. I rolled forward off the table and grabbed my right hand, still holding the nail with my left, and swung upward into his crotch, once, twice, three times, almost as fast as Ozzie.

Two-Ray doubled over, cupping his balls with his bleeding hand, trying to raise the Glock. I stepped inside his gun arm, thrusting upward with the heel of my left hand into his chin to snap his head back. With my right hand, I jammed the nail into his neck, aiming for the jugular. Two-Ray's hand went up to grab mine. Then the nail went through to something soft, and his blood sprayed like a fountain on me, on the floor.

Two-Ray dropped the gun and fell back on the concrete

floor, his eyes wide, his mouth open. He tried to say something, probably "You bitch!" but it came out as a bloody gargle. I stepped back, but somehow he got to his feet and staggered toward me, reaching for the knife at his side. His other hand was on his neck, trying to stop the blood that gushed through his fingers. He stood there wavering like a tree in the wind. Then he fell toward me. I spun to the side as he came crashing down, splintering the table into firewood.

I took a deep breath. My heart was, strangely, beating normally. I looked down at the dead giant, blood no longer spurting but oozing from his neck. His head was turned to one side, his eyes half-open. My stomach grumbled.

I went over to help CC get up. He screamed when I took his arm. "No! It's broken!" I gently grabbed his other shoulder and boosted him to his feet.

CC hobbled to a chair and sat down. He stared at Two-Ray's body, his eyes wide. "You killed him."

Yes, I did. Time to think about that later. "I'm going to check upstairs. The other two will be coming back soon. We have to get out of here."

I picked up the Glock from the floor and jacked a round into the chamber, then went out into the hallway and up the stairs. Next to the Escalade was a table with two plastic bags: one held dozens of bundles of green-and-white capsules wrapped in plastic, the other, cash. I took both bags then headed to the stairs.

Tucking the bags under my belt, I grabbed a gas can sitting next to the Caddy. I passed a filthy sink with a cracked mirror above it. I saw myself covered in blood, like Carrie as prom queen. I couldn't do anything about the clothes, but I washed my hands and face then went back downstairs.

As I walked in the door, a bright flash blinded me. I had my finger on the Glock's trigger before I could see again. CC was holding an iPhone and taking pictures of the body.

I tucked the gun in my jeans. *I know, Grandpa, I set the safety.* I snatched the phone out of his hands. "I almost shot you. What the hell are you doing? Where'd you get this?"

"This is his phone," he said, pointing to the dead Two-Ray. "I sent the pictures to myself. I want always to remember who was my mother's killer."

I took Two-Ray's phone, deleted the photos, and stuck it in my pocket. There might be some useful numbers in it.

"Our DNA and our fingerprints are all over. We've got to burn this place," I said, handing him the gas can. CC took it and, leaning against a metal post, started splashing gas around. I put the plastic bag with the drugs in the middle of the floor next to Two-Ray's body. I put my wallet back in my bag and grabbed my Princeton hoodie that CC had been wearing.

Suddenly I was weak. I leaned against the wall before I fell down. My stomach started churning, and I felt a burning sensation in my gut. I tasted something sour, and I leaned over and puked. And puked and puked. I dropped to my knees, retching and retching, until nothing more came out.

I had killed a man. He was a rapist, a drug dealer, and a murderer, and he was going to kill me and CC, but my stomach didn't care. Grandpa did say that there were consequences. I wondered if he'd ever vomited afterward. I swallowed, the bitter taste burning my throat.

CC tossed the gas can in a corner and looked over at me. "Are you OK?"

I nodded and got up. I helped CC up the stairs and

outside. Then I went back down to the little room that smelled of gasoline. I found a glass pipe and some matches on the floor among the pieces of the shattered table. I lit a match, put it to the matchbook, and tossed it. The gasoline ignited, and the flames spread quickly.

I ran up the stairs and took CC's good arm. We went out the front door, headed for the corner. Just then, I heard a shout behind me. Duane and the other guy were half a block away and running toward us. I yanked the Glock from my waistband and pushed CC around the corner of the building. Flames were coming up the stairs and out of the open door.

"Wait here."

I ducked behind a telephone pole and aimed the Glock, but in the dark street, I didn't have much of a shot.

What is the weapon, Deborah?

A Glock 19 Parabellum, Grandpa.

Not like the Nagant. It has a recoil. Adjust for it.

I know, Grandpa.

Calculate. Not where the target is now but where it is going to be.

Wayne and Duane were getting closer. Wayne five-ten, blue Knicks jersey, in the lead; Duane, six feet or so, to his right. I took Grandpa's shooting stance—body sideways, left hand over right—remembering not to squeeze the grip. I fired twice, aiming high. I didn't want to kill them.

They ducked behind a parked car. A second later, they started shooting, but the bullets went everywhere except near me. I crouched and hurried around the corner where CC was leaning against the building, then ran to the Buick and opened the door. "Get in!" Crossing my fingers, I turned the key. Good old reliable Buick. We drove off, and I managed to burn rubber as we sped away.

We stopped at CC's apartment on Seventh Street, where he sat in the car while I retrieved the key under the doormat, opened it, and put the cash on the couch. We went back outside and headed off again.

"I left you a lot of cash. You're going to have to leave town. Do you have any friends, family somewhere?"

CC nodded. "A cousin. In California."

"Go there. But don't go to La Guardia or Kennedy. Cops might be looking for you. Get a plane from Philly or Newark. As soon as you can. Do not tell anyone where you're going. But let's get you patched up."

I drove fast to New York Hospital on O Street. I parked behind a dumpster, put on my sweatshirt inside out, and pulled the hood up in case of cameras. Then I ran to the emergency door, grabbed a wheelchair, and pushed it back to the car. CC managed to get himself halfway out of the car, and I boosted him into the chair.

At the entrance, I knelt in front of CC. I grabbed his chin and made him look at me. "Listen. When the cops question you, tell them somebody attacked you and you woke up sitting here. You don't know how you got here." I paused. "What did I say?"

"I got attacked. I woke up here. I don't know how I got here."

I gave him a kiss on his puffed and bloody lips.

He winced, then smiled at me. "Thank you."

I went back to the Buick, unloaded the Glock, wiped it, and threw it into the dumpster before I drove off.

ॐॐॐ

My mouth still tasted like vomit. I parked on Coney Island Avenue and walked across the street to an all-night bodega. Inside, I nodded at the Sikh with a black turban and big beard behind the counter. I went to the back to the cooler section. I needed something to get the taste out.

On the bottom shelf of the cooler was this lone bottle: Vernor's Ginger Ale. What the heck. Give it a try. The Sikh took my money, handed me an opener. On the way to the car, I took a swig.

Wow. I'd never tasted anything like this before. Sweet, but with a sharp edge. Real ginger, maybe. Whatever it was, it worked. No more vomit taste. I drove back to Brighton Beach, to Second Street, to my home.

ॐॐॐ

I went upstairs and showered, brushed my teeth twice, and rinsed with an awful tasting mouthwash. I dressed, stuffed my blood-soaked clothes in the backyard barbecue, and burned them to ashes. I went to bed, the streetlight shining on the she-wolf picture. I slept without dreams of running, without seeing someone behind a fence, without any dreams at all.

CHAPTER

I woke up as the sun came through my bedroom window, hearing Grandma and Grandpa.

To take a life, it is wrong. It is a sin.

Even to save your own life?

Thou shall not kill. God makes no exceptions.

Deborah, our granddaughter, she saved a life. And her own life.

What about the price you paid, the cost to you and to me? There is always another way.

I got out of bed and went downstairs. I couldn't help but look in the dining room, half-expecting to see Grandma and Grandpa at the table. Let them argue it out, decide if I was going to hell or not.

My stomach grumbled, and I realized, a little surprised, that I was hungry. I went down to the kosher bakery on Ocean and had orange juice, coffee, and a bagel. Heading out the door, I passed a newspaper rack and saw a copy of the *Post*. On the cover, a full-page color photo: the burning warehouse in Ozone Park. The headline: Drug Dealer Smoked. At the bottom of the page was an inset photo. Two-Ray's bloody body on the floor and me from the waist down. A pair of legs—my legs—in holey jeans and black Louboutin boots, a hand—my hand—holding the Glock 19. The text, all in caps: "The Killer?" It was CC's photo. Holy crap. I bought a copy and went home, looking over my shoulder.

The article didn't say much: suspected drug kingpin dead, photo of his maybe-possibly-likely killer from an anonymous source, police investigating possible turf war with another drug gang. Were there cameras around the warehouse I didn't notice? What about cameras at the hospital? I wished I had a passport. If I ever saw CC again, I was going to... well, not kill him, but give him a talking-to.

࿔࿔࿔

"Are you all right?" Becky's first words when I called her.

"Yes. No. I don't know."

"I'll come over."

I looked out the window as Becky pulled up in her Beemer. She carried her laptop.

"I made coffee," I said, heading to the kitchen.

We sat down at the dining room table, and I made sure to put coasters down for our cups. Grandma would have a fit if the wood had a ring on it.

Becky sat down and took a sip of coffee. "So. What's going on?"

I got up from the table and started to the kitchen. "Would you like a semi-fresh brownie?"

"There's something you're not telling me," she said.

Two-Ray's dead face took over my vision for a moment. I had to tell her. I had to tell somebody. I paced back and forth in the dining room, Becky growing more curious. I sat down across from her.

"Remember when I asked Ethan to find the owner of a car?" I began. Somewhere in the telling I saw the body on the cement floor. I smelled the burning wood and flesh. My stomach began to churn as if it were happening again. I showed her my picture on the *Post* cover. "That's me," I said, "I killed him." I told her the whole story.

Becky's mouth had been open for the last two minutes when I finally finished. "*Ihe dị nsọ!*" she said.

"What does that mean?" I asked. Becky didn't answer. She got up, her chair scraping across the wooden floor. Without a word, she picked up her bag and walked to the door. She was leaving. I'd lost her, like I'd lost Ozzie.

At the door, Becky stopped and put her hand on the wall, like she was afraid of falling. Then she turned back to me. "There's something I didn't tell you." She came back to the dining room. "After my family was killed, I was angry. I stopped going to classes, stopped seeing friends, and turned away from people who wanted to help me.

"I could only think about what had happened to my parents and my little sister," she said. "I could only think about going back to Nigeria, finding the men who killed my family. I started doing research on Boko Haram. In England I had friends at school who taught me things. I learned how to break encryption, steal passwords." Becky looked out the window over my shoulder, staring into her past.

"Every day I searched the Boko Haram files, thinking I might learn about them." Becky turned back to me, tears running down her cheeks. "They had places on the dark web. They liked to brag about the women they'd turned into sex slaves, about the children they'd turned into soldiers, about their killings. I found the group that had been in our area, and they talked about the raid on our town." Becky wiped tears from her eyes. "My father had friends in the government, people who might do something. I sent them the information I'd collected." Becky shook her head. "I waited and waited. No one replied. I never heard a thing."

She sighed. "I got even angrier. I found a gun dealer in Oyo. I bought a plane ticket to Lagos, I went to the airport. But I couldn't board the plane. I was afraid." She held up her arm, the bracelets sliding down to reveal the scar. "That's when…" She put her head down, her tears falling onto the dining room table. "When you told me what had happened, with that drug dealer, I was jealous. I was angry—at myself."

I reached across the table, putting my hand on hers. "It's not the same thing. I was fighting for my life. If you had gone back to hunt those men, you would have been killed," I said. I took a breath. "When I moved to the city, did all those drugs, I told myself I was doing a good thing, staying away so you and Ethan wouldn't be in danger. But I think I wanted to die too."

Becky took her laptop out of her bag. "Let's see if there is any more news about this." She booted the laptop. I went to look over her shoulder. Nope. Nothing new. "You're still the mystery killer," she said, with a little smile. She thought for a moment. "The only thing is, those boots. Some clever policeman, or more likely a policewoman, might start checking sales of, what? Gucci? Louboutin?"

"Louboutin. I bought them in the city. I paid cash," I said.

"OK. But be careful where you wear them. Too bad. They're nice." She looked down at my feet then back at me. With a half-smile, she said, "What size are they?"

Despite myself, I laughed out loud. "There's a name for people like you!"

"Yes. Enterprising." We both laughed.

Becky closed her laptop, put it in her bag, and got up. "Ethan and I are going to Cleveland to visit my aunt and uncle. We will be safe." She squeezed my arm and raised her eyebrows. "You are strong—strong enough to pursue this."

"Thank you. Oh yeah, what does '*ihe dị nsọ'* mean?" I asked.

"It's my language. Igbo. A rough translation is 'holy shit.'" It made me smile. She went down the steps then turned back. "Text me if you need help on those codes."

We went out to the porch and hugged, then Becky got into her car and drove away. I crossed my fingers for her and my brother. I was stronger. I was getting better. It was nothing like I thought closure was supposed to be, but something else, maybe. Something that had been loosened in me. My arms tensed up as I remembered fighting the man who was going to kill me. Second-place Deb would have been killed, but I'd won.

I could certainly decipher Grandpa's secret code.

I turned to go back inside and saw a brown envelope sticking out of our little mailbox. My name on it, no postage or return address. I squeezed it; there was something small and flat inside, probably not a bomb.

I sat down at the dining room table to open it. I took out a DVD and a slip of paper.

Deborah,

Thank you again for saving me. Sorry about the picture. I sent it to my cousin, and he put it on Snapchat. Am on my way to the airport. The police came to the hospital and asked questions, but I didn't know anything :-)

The disk was in the bag with the $$. Maybe it's about drug dealing or something.

Carlos-Charlie/CC

I went up to my room, got my laptop, and took it down to Grandpa's office. As I sat in his old, squeaky chair, I smiled, remembering the hundreds of times I'd heard that sound. I put the disk in the drive. A title appeared: Teacher's Pet. I was thinking it was an old Disney movie—for about five seconds.

A girl with long blond hair, about six or seven, sat on a desk in a classroom: a blackboard, colored artwork on the walls. A man wearing a mask came into the room. The girl looked frightened. The man stroked her hair with one hand, put his other hand on her skirted leg. I hit the Eject button. I felt like puking again. Two-Ray was a murderer who dealt drugs and kiddy porn. I wanted to kill him again. I threw the disk in the trash.

I had to get it out of my system. I went running. Three miles around the neighborhood, then I came home and showered for a long time. I dug out the ledger scans and Father Andy's translations from my laundry pile then took them into Grandpa's office.

Peter. John. James. Samuel. Koloman. Matthew. Five, six, and seven. Forty-six ledger entries, from February to May. Nothing to connect them to anything. I thought about texting Becky, but felt like I'd be admitting failure after two hours. I'd read the Old and New Testament books online; no help. Lots of begats, killings, and miracles, but no answers.

I browsed Grandpa's *A History of Kievan Rus'*. Koloman of Hungary was the first king of Galicia-Volhynia in the thirteenth century, a kingdom that included the Land of Kviv, which became Ukraine. So what?

I put the book back on Grandpa's shelf, shoving the other books to one side. A worn leather-bound Bible, Grandpa's Bible, fell to the floor behind his desk. I picked it up. On the inside cover, in Grandpa's tiny but neat handwriting, Віктор Соколов, Одеса, *1973*. Viktor Sokolov, Odessa, 1973.

Grandma used to quiz Ethan and me on the names of the Bible books. We'd have a contest who could say them faster. Then Ethan came up with "Matthew, Mark, Doc and Sneezy," and we fell on the floor laughing. Grandma, disgusted, would get up and stomp into the kitchen, muttering, "*hrikh i spokusa.*"

A corner of the table of contents page was folded, and I straightened it out. *Buttya, Vykhid, Levyt:* Genesis, Exodus, Leviticus…I noticed a tiny red dot next to I Kings.

I Kings. Koloman was the first king.

I turned to I Kings. Chapter 3, verse nine had a number written in red ink in the margin: $7,500. Chapter 4, verse eleven: $43,325 and $77,204.

I pulled out the scans of the ledger entries: there were Glagolitic entries for Koloman on March 9 and April 11.

It took me another hour to check all the entries. "Five, six, seven" turned out to be the book of Numbers. The forty-six ledger entries with Glagolitic notations pointed to books, chapters, and verses in Grandpa's Bible. The amounts he'd written in the Bible added up to a little over five million dollars.

Grandpa had made notes of East-West Imports' problem transactions in his Bible, pointing to them in his ledger in an obscure language that looked like doodles. He knew someone—maybe one of Uncle Teddy's Russian partners— was embezzling from the *orhanizatsiyi*. On that Thursday in May, he made a ledger entry: $973,600. On that Thursday in May, he warned Uncle Teddy. Friday night, he and Grandma were murdered.

Grandpa was so smart. Smart enough to make a code, put entries in a Bible, hide it and the ledger in the garage. Just not smart enough to know that someone would find out what he knew and come for him and Grandma. I leaned back in Grandpa's squeaky chair, tears running down my face. But they weren't sad tears. They burned. My old friends, the shards of glass, the shrapnel, came back, poking at me. *Do something. Do something.*

I don't remember going to my room, taking the Nagant box from under my bed, and bringing it downstairs. I stood at the bottom of the stairs, holding the pistol. The grip felt cool in my hand. I remembered my dreams of running, of someone behind a fence. I pointed the Nagant at the door. I am *vovchytsya*.

My stomach churned. But I didn't care. Someone killed my grandparents. Someone had to pay.

వ్ వ్ వ్

I called Uncle Teddy at East-West Imports. I drove there in Grandpa's Buick, then went up the stairs to Uncle Teddy's office. I carried Grandpa's old briefcase with scans of the ledger, the Bible entries, and a printout of the transactions. The Nagant was in my jacket.

Olek, talking to a bearded guy in a too-tight suit, came over.

"I never got the chance to tell you how sorry I was, Deborah," he said, hugging me for a little too long, squeezing a little too tightly. "If there's anything I can do..." He smiled, showing the gap in his front teeth. He pointed to the briefcase. "That was Viktor's? What's in it?"

"Something for your father," I said and went upstairs.

Uncle Teddy, sitting at his gray metal desk, beckoned to me when he saw me through the glass door.

"Sit down, Deborah," Uncle Teddy said, pointing to a green upholstered chair. "You were very mysterious on your phone call," he said, smiling. "What have you found?"

I didn't sit. I opened the briefcase and laid the pages on his desk. It took two minutes to show him everything. Uncle Teddy stared at the papers then looked at me. For the first time I'd ever seen, Uncle Teddy wasn't a man in control; he was an old man, everything he thought he knew dissolving, fading away. He turned pale, opened and closed his mouth.

"There must be some explanation..." He stared at the pages, hoping to find it there.

"There is," I said. "You know there was money missing. Grandpa kept your books. He found the shady transactions and was going to find out more. That's why he and Grandma were murdered."

"But Pavluk—" he began.

"Pavluk didn't kill them!" I yelled at him.

"How do you know?"

"Because someone searched the house—my house— looking for the ledger. Pavluk is in prison."

Uncle Teddy shook his head, looking out the dirty windows to the river. "I will look into this."

"Do you remember what Grandpa told you? 'You will not have far to look.'"

Uncle Teddy looked up at me, almost smiling. "That night—you were listening."

"Yeah. Guilty," I said. I closed Grandpa's briefcase and headed to the door.

Uncle Teddy called after me, "Deborah. Wait."

I turned back to him. He wiped his face and ran his hands through his hair, trying to pull it together. "This…" He pointed to the papers on his desk. "It can be dangerous. Be careful."

"I'm through being careful, Teo." I'd never called him that before. "Whoever stole from you killed Grandpa and Grandma to cover it up. I'm going to find him." Words welled up, unleashed from a hole deep inside me: *And I'm going to kill him.* But I couldn't say them.

Vovchytsya.

Uncle Teddy stared at me, his mouth open.

I went out and down the narrow hall to Grandpa's office. Grandpa's old desk and chair were still there. I straightened the ink-stained blotter and moved the dusty brass lamp to a corner of the desk, straightening things out for Grandpa. I stacked the clutter of old papers, invoices, and notes he'd made to himself that he'd never, ever read. I sat in his chair, looking through the dirty window at the river, watching a sailboat.

Then I heard Uncle Teddy call, "Olek! Come here!"

Olek walked by, not seeing me, and went into Uncle Teddy's office. I thought I'd stay a bit longer. I duckwalked over to the wall separating Grandpa's office from Teo's and listened.

"Five million dollars," I heard Uncle Teddy say. "Gone."

Olek's voice, raised, angry: "Our business is failing. The Russians, the Armenians, they are taking over, no matter how many meetings we have. We must change, Teo. If you had done what I wanted to do—"

"That is not the business we're in, Oleksandr," Uncle Teddy said. "It will never be our business. We have rules—rules we made before you were born."

Olek made a spitting noise. "Rules! You sit here and make rules, make phone calls, make deals, and we've lost control of our business!"

I ducked below the partition in Grandpa's office as Olek came out, banging the door against the wall as he walked through. "Let me make the rules! I'll do better than you!" Uncle Teddy's office door slammed shut, rattling the glass.

As Olek stomped down the hall, I heard Uncle Teddy yell, "Volodymyr! Volodymyr!" Hurrying footsteps came up the stairs. Out the window I saw Olek's red Hummer drive away, spitting gravel. I went downstairs, got into the old Buick, and drove home, starting to breathe normally.

The shit was gonna hit the fan. A growing part of me was hoping it happened soon.

I spent an hour going through the stack of newspapers in the garage, hoping that Grandpa had hidden something else. No luck. Whatever else he might have found out, either it wasn't on paper or it was taken by the killer. Then I spread out a newspaper on Grandpa's desk, took out the Nagant, and cleaned and reloaded it.

How many rounds, Deborah?

Seven rounds, Grandpa. Seven point-sixty-two by thirty-eight-millimeter caliber.

Accuracy?

Best at under twenty-five feet. Fifty if I'm good.
Are you good?
I am, Grandpa. I'm very good.

I heard a step on the porch and jumped up, grabbing the Nagant. Then I heard Mrs. Krasny's voice say, "Deborah, are you there?"

I put the gun in the desk drawer and went to greet her. She had a worried look on her face. "I thought I heard you come home," she said. "Are you alright?"

I held the door open. "Come in, Mrs. Krasny. I'm fine." I turned to go into the kitchen. "Can I get you something?"

"No dear. I'm inviting you over. I found some things tucked away. I thought you might want to see them. And you can stay for dinner."

I started to say no but didn't have the heart. She really wanted to help. I could see my house from her living room anyway.

৯৯৯

The Krasny kitchen smelled of cabbage, which brought back some memories I'd tried to forget. But time maybe, or just a callus over the shrapnel, made it OK. Mr. Krasny's truck pulled up in front and he came in wearing his blue Krasny Automotive overalls.

"Go change and wash, Yakov," Mrs. Krasny said. "You smell like automobiles."

We sat down to iced tea, cabbage soup with sausage, and homemade bread. I'd been eating Aunt Elena's frozen entrees, ramen, or takeout, for a month, so this was good. More memories.

I was able to talk about Grandpa and Grandma without feeling like crying. The Krasnys remembered me as a little girl, when I'd first come to live next door, and I laughed when Mrs. Krasny told a story about how, many summers ago, I'd run too fast onto the Slip 'N Slide and wound up in the rose bushes. Grandma couldn't decide if she was more concerned about me or her roses.

I offered to help Mrs. Krasny clean up, but she shooed me away. Mr. Krasny beckoned. "Come and see. I have some pictures of your family from a long time ago."

We went into the living room, and Mr. Krasny took out a leatherbound album. Inside were pictures of my grandparents posing with a young couple smiling in the front yard. "Your parents, long before you and Ethan." I'd seen some of these before, but I was glad to look at them again.

Mr. Krasny glanced into the kitchen, closed the album, and turned to me. In a low voice, he said, "Anna doesn't want me to talk with you about this. But I know you are not happy. You should know. Maybe it's something."

He got up and put the album away. "That night," he began, then cleared his throat. "That night, I told you I heard a car driving away, and I saw the fire. But I was mistaken," he said. "I remembered. I was awake in bed when the car—a powerful car—drove away. You know, on our street, there are no cars that late." He sat down next to me. "It was later, when I got up to go to the bathroom, I looked out the window and saw the flames."

It took me a minute. Mr. Krasny peered into my face, worried that he'd said too much.

"You heard the car *before* you saw the fire?"

He nodded. "Maybe fifteen, twenty minutes."

The police report had it wrong. My grandparents had been killed before the fire started. I had been looking at Gorodsky's security camera footage after the fire. If the killer had set some kind of trigger or timer, he'd have been long gone when it went off. I had to take another look at the video.

I stood up. "I thank you, Mr. Krasny," I said, taking his hands in mine. "I'll go to the police with this." I smiled, nodding toward the kitchen. "I promise not to tell Anna."

He looked relieved. "She says you shouldn't keep thinking about what happened. But I know you will never forget."

ớ ớ ớ

I plugged the flash drive into my laptop, fast-forwarding through the week of days and nights, waiting and waiting. Then there it was: 05-14, 11:07 p.m. A black SUV, maybe a Caddy or GMC, no front license plate, turned left from Second onto Ocean. The driver's side visor was down; all I could see was an arm in a black shirt or jacket. The image was blurry; he was driving fast. Not much help.

I paused the video, staring at the screen. Too small. I clicked around until I found a way to blow up the image. I figured how to save the video frame as an image then tried to enlarge it, but it got all pixelated. Becky would know how to make it clearer. But she and Ethan needed to be safe.

I saw something that might be a dent in the front fender and a blurry streak on the passenger side windshield. The streak might be something on the passenger seatback or a reflection on the glass from something on the street. I went back to the video and examined it frame by frame. The SUV moved forward, the streak along with it.

I leaned back, rubbing my eyes, glancing again out of the window to the street. Not much to go on. There were probably a thousand cars like that in Brooklyn, but five or six of them were at the *orhanizatsiyi´s* warehouse. I copied the video to my phone and decided to head back to the warehouse to look for the black SUV. It was late, and there'd be no one there. But I had Grandpa's key. I stuck the Nagant in my jacket.

CHAPTER 17

I backed the Buick out of the driveway and headed to Ocean to get on the Belt Parkway. As I turned right onto Ocean, I looked in my rearview mirror to see a car behind me, blue and white lights on the roof, flashing its headlights.

It was Boris again, probably wondering what I was doing out so late. I pulled over, and he parked behind me. I had to squint due to the bright headlights as I looked in the sideview mirror. The cop car door opened, and in the other side mirror, I saw the passenger side door open and someone else get out.

In the driver's side mirror, I saw the guy coming toward me. He was short and fat, and he had a gun in his hand. Not Boris. Not a cop.

I slammed the gearshift into drive and stepped on the gas, swinging the wheel wildly to miss a parked car in front of me. I heard two shots and saw the guys running back to the car.

I skidded right onto Coney Island Avenue then realized my mistake. I was going to run out of road in two blocks. In my mirror I saw the car, its lights flashing, gaining on me. There was no way this Buick was going to outrun them. A loud crack, and a bullet hit the rear window, shattering the glass and thudding into the dashboard. I swung the wheel and sideswiped a car as I turned right again onto a street. This was my neighborhood, but I'd never had to get away from murderers before.

Another shot. I started swerving back and forth, then swung into the big apartment block on Oceana. Maybe they didn't know the neighborhood.

Left onto Seacoast, my foot to the floor, the Buick's engine maxed out. They were right behind. Left onto Brighton Beach Avenue—and then they rammed me. The car skidded sideways and slammed into a dumpster at the curb. I bounced off the steering wheel and back against the seat. I looked over my shoulder and saw the cop car park behind me. I reached for the gun, but it had fallen out of my jacket onto the floor. I'd be dead before I could get it. I fumbled for the seatbelt. I could run up the block and into a building. Or I could dash across the street to the park, maybe lose them.

Or I could die right here. But God, or fate, or Grandpa, was with me. That old Buick was still running. I backed up and headed right for the fat guy with the gun, and he fell to the street to get out of the way. The other guy, skinnier, took aim but fired high. I kept going until I'd slammed into the cop car, which skidded backward. I hit a parked car behind me and the Buick bounced up on the curb. I shifted into drive and took off.

Where the hell were real cops? If those guys were real cops, I'd be public enemy number one.

They knew where I lived, but I guessed—hoped—they didn't know their way around. I drove to Ocean View, where I'd seen an empty house for sale. I pulled into the driveway and swung onto the backyard grass, where I parked out of sight from the street. I found the Nagant under the driver's seat. Ducking behind cars and bushes every time I saw headlights, I headed home. I walked up Brighton First path and up the narrow walkway between two houses, then climbed over the fence from the Krasnys' and into my yard. I ducked behind a trashcan as the cop car, its front bumper hanging down, cruised slowly up my street.

I opened the back door and listened for anyone who might be waiting in my house. My house. After a minute I got the ledger and the scans from the freezer and stuffed them in a trash bag. I went the front door. I looked up and down my street then went over to the Krasnys' and tucked the documents under the front porch. I left the neighborhood the way I'd come in.

The Q was almost empty except for an angry-looking woman in medical scrubs with cornrows, and a drunk flopped across the seats. I kept my hand on the Nagant in my jacket, squeezing the grip every time the train stopped. I wiped sweat from my face.

At DeKalb, I switched to the R, ducking behind pillars and looking behind me to see if anyone was following.

I caught a cab from South Ferry to Penn Station, almost empty at two a.m. I wandered down though the aisle of little shops, KFC, Domino's Pizza, Shake Shack, all closed. But I wasn't hungry.

I went up the escalator and saw two cops coming down. My hand went to the Nagant in my bag, but they weren't fat and skinny, and they ignored me. I laughed at myself. A shootout with cops. Right!

I went back up to the main concourse, my head swiveling

like I was watching a tennis match. Everyone coming in the glass doors began to look like a Ukrainian or a Russian gangster, somebody who wanted me dead.

I found a cab with a sleepy driver on Sixth Avenue and had him drop me off on Broome. It was still dark, with only a few drunks and night owls on the street. I walked fast, but not too fast, putting my hood up and my hand on the Nagant. No one paid me any attention, but you never know. I walked to Elizabeth Street and my apartment, my last safe space. No one was looking for Deborah Sturm. I flopped on my unmade bed, too tired to take off my clothes. I fell asleep in a minute.

CHAPTER 18

I was dreaming of the wooden fence again, but I wasn't running, just facing it. Someone I couldn't see was scratching on it. Then I woke up. The scratching was real and coming from outside the door. I got up, grabbed the Nagant, and crept across the floor in the darkened room. Wait for whoever to pick the lock, or surprise him?

I chose door number two. I unlocked the door as quietly as I could and swung it wide, aiming the Nagant.

A tall, thin guy with a shaved head reacted quickly. He grabbed my wrist and twisted it, forcing me to drop the gun. He shoved me hard, and I staggered back into the room, off-balance. He stepped in and closed the door. I scrambled in the dark, looking for the pistol, but he slammed his foot down on me, holding me. He reached into his gray leather jacket for what I was sure was a gun.

I seized his leg and twisted it as hard as I could, getting up to my knees at the same time. He tried to pull his leg free. I stood up, stepped to him, and jammed my Louboutin-shod foot down hard on his instep. He grunted and staggered back. I let go of his leg and stepped forward to grab him by the neck with both hands and pull his face down to my raised knee. He was expecting that. He put his hands across his face, shoving hard at my knee and throwing me off-balance. He came toward me. I picked up my bag and threw it at him, but he ducked and swung his fist up to my face. I stepped to one side and grabbed his fist, twisting as hard as I could.

But he was good—as good as Ozzie. He bent down as I pulled away, then swung his free hand into my stomach. I bent over double, gasping. Just in time I saw the blackjack in his left hand as he swung it at me. I twisted my body away, and it hit me on the shoulder. My arm went limp and a wave of pain shot down to my fingers.

The guy bent low, charged at me, and knocked me backward onto the floor. He jumped on top of me, pinning my arms to the floor under his knees.

"*Malen'kaya suchka!*" he said in Russian, close enough to Ukrainian: "little bitch." He took a hypodermic syringe—not a gun—out of his jacket and smiled. "Too bad about your drug habit," he said, grinning. "Overdoses are so common."

He leaned forward. I raised my legs, wrapped them around his head, and pulled with all my strength. He fell backward, dropping the syringe. He grabbed at my legs, trying to pull them apart. I rolled to my side, and he fell, still in my legs' grip. But he was reaching out, trying to grab the syringe. He took hold of it then swung his leg over and thumped me in the stomach. I couldn't hold him with my legs. I almost couldn't breathe. He sat astride me again, shoving my head to one side, uncapping the syringe with his teeth.

As he spit out the cap, I grabbed his wrist with both my hands and shoved. The needle went into his eye, and I pushed the plunger. He screamed in pain and fell away from me, reaching to pull the needle out.

I scrambled to my feet and backed away. The hands of the man who came to kill me fluttered like the wings of a wounded bird, growing weaker and weaker. His legs shook and bounced up and down on the wooden floor as if they were on springs. His head rolled to one side, his legs stopped bouncing, his hands stopped flapping and flopped to the floor. He went limp and his eyes grew wider, then his head turned to one side to gaze away into that distance only the dying can see.

I rolled away, feeling the pain in my shoulder and stomach. I sat on the floor taking deep breaths. I remembered Ozzie's advice: "Take care of your breath, and it will take care of you." I got to my feet, staggered into the kitchen, and upchucked into the sink, the bile burning my throat. I'd killed again, and my internal argument—*He was going to kill you*—didn't help much. Grandma was silent, but I felt her watching. I turned on the water to wash away the puke, then washed my face and hands. I swallowed some water and spit some out. I got a bottle of Vernor's out of the fridge, opened it, and took a drink.

I went back to the living room, retrieved the Nagant and sat on the floor. I'd gotten too close to answers that my grandparents' killer didn't want me to have. But I wasn't safe here, even in my so-called secret hideaway. The old me would have felt frightened, shaken. But the she-wolf would fight when cornered. Fight to the death.

On my floor was a dead man. It had been a person once. Now it was just an empty thing. No more promises, no more dreams. I wondered if he had a wife and kids waiting for him somewhere. I felt sorry for them, not for him. I'd obsessed about Two-Ray and the others, wondering if I could have done something differently, if I could have wounded him, if I could have knocked him out, disabled him long enough to escape.

No second-guessing—not now, not ever. *This would-be killer on my floor was sent by someone who murdered my grandparents,* I thought, *and who wants me dead. I will kill him before he kills me. I am the she-wolf.*

I noticed for the first time a scattering of little white pills on the floor next to a cracked plastic pill bottle.

"Ozzie. Please come. I need help," I said into my phone.

Ten minutes later there was a knock at the door. I had the Nagant aimed at the door before I heard Ozzie. "It's me," he said. He came in, saw the body, and looked at me. I told him about the fake cops and the man, dead on the floor, who'd tried to kill me. "Who wants you dead?"

"I'll tell you. But can we deal with this?" I replied, pointing to the guy on the floor.

Ozzie went over and picked up the pills and the syringe. "They wanted to make it look like you were a junkie who OD'ed."

"I figured out that part," I said. "But I don't know how they found me. I made sure I wasn't followed, and I used another name to rent this place."

Ozzie pointed to my hand, clutching the phone. "Who has your phone number?"

Oh crap. Ethan, Becky, Uncle Teddy, Voly, Mrs. Krasny, Aunt Elena—everybody. I felt stupid. I'd spent hours changing trains, taking a cab, ducking into side streets, looking over my shoulder, and they'd been following me from the comfort of their living room. Or wherever. Ozzie took the phone and went into the bathroom. I heard a splash.

Ozzie came back and knelt next to the body to search through the pockets. "No ID. Just a phone."

Ozzie opened the call list. He punched in a number on the call list and put the cell on speaker. A gravelly, accented voice spoke. "Is it finished?"

Ozzie looked over at me. It was not a voice I knew. I shrugged, shaking my head.

"*Sergey. Gotovo*? Sergei. Is it done?"

Ozzie clicked off and broke the phone in half. He went to my kitchen, rummaged around in the cabinets, and pulled out two plastic trash bags. "Use these," he said, pointing to the dead guy who used to be Sergei.

I was on autopilot, not letting myself think about what we were doing. We pulled the bags over the body, one on the legs, the other over the head and shoulders. Ozzie grabbed the body by the shoulders and dragged it to the door. "Give me a hand."

I opened my door and looked out. The hallway was empty. I grabbed the guy's legs, and we carried him—or it—into the hallway.

Ozzie looked around. "Is there a rear door?" he whispered. I nodded, and we carried the body down the narrow hallway to a fire door. I propped it open, checking the alley for people or lights from windows.

We propped it against the wall. Ozzie put the pill bottle in Sergei's pocket and stuck the plastic bags and the syringe in a dumpster. "Get what you need. We have to go."

I went back to my apartment and took what I needed: the Nagant.

CHAPTER

I walked to the street, but Ozzie stopped me. "There's a car parked in front of your building. Someone's in it—probably the guy on the phone. Three cars down. A black Caddy. Tinted windows. "My van's across the street."

We stepped out from behind the building to see a big, bearded guy going up the stairs of my apartment building. He turned, saw us, and drew a gun from his belt. The part of my brain not occupied with staying alive noticed that it was Ruger nine-millimeter, with a noise suppressor and seventeen-round magazine.

"Run!" Ozzie said.

We dashed across the street, and I heard a clink!—a bullet hitting the light pole on the corner. Two more silenced plinks hit the car I ducked behind. Ozzie was behind me. I stuck my head up to see the guy running toward us. I gripped my Nagant.

How many rounds?

Seven, Grandpa.

Accuracy?

Fifty feet if I'm very good. Ten if I'm just OK.

I aimed to the bearded guy's left and fired. The round hit

the wall of a building, splintering brick, the noise startling me and him. He stopped and ducked behind a car at the corner then stood up to fire three more shots. Eleven more rounds, twelve if he'd had one in the chamber. I fired three more shots, none anywhere near the target.

I heard a noise behind me and took a look. Ozzie was holding the open door of a rusty white van. Behind us, I heard a car starting. We got in and ducked down as the Caddy squealed around the corner and past us. I stuck my head up to see the bearded guy swiveling his head side to side, looking for us. Ozzie started up the van and followed behind, his lights out. He turned left on Bowery, blending in with early-morning traffic.

We drove for a mile or so, then Ozzie bent forward, his head almost hitting the steering wheel. He jammed on the brakes, throwing me forward, and I saw blood on the seat back behind him.

"You're hit!" I cried. Ozzie straightened up, and I saw the blood on his left arm. A car honked at us. I jumped out and ran to the driver's side, waving the honking car around us. "Can you walk?"

Ozzie nodded, struggling to get out. I took his arm to help. He yelled. "Sorry." I took his right arm and helped him to the passenger side and into the passenger seat, then got in to drive. "We're going to the hospital."

Ozzie reached over with his right hand and gripped my arm like a vise. "No hospital. Just drive. I'll tell you where."

We pulled into a dirt parking lot somewhere on the West Side as the sun came up behind us. Ozzie pointed, and I parked the van next to a row of cargo containers. Ozzie opened his door and beckoned to me.

He limped down the row, holding his hand over his bloody arm. He stopped at a container, unlocked the padlock, and opened the squeaky metal door.

It was an apartment, almost as big as the one I had: a rusty cot, folding table, electric one-burner cooker, a tiny fridge next to a wooden three-drawer cabinet, a lamp, two metal chairs, and an old armchair with the stuffing coming out. A pipe-frame rack with some clothes on it. A bookshelf with a row of books. An extension cord duct-taped to the wall exited out a hole in the metal side.

Ozzie went to the cot and fell on it, groaning. He pointed and said, "Alcohol, bandages, sutures. In the cabinet."

I'd never done this before. I couldn't do it. But somehow, I did. I cut off his shirt, trying not to touch the bullet wound. "Pour the alcohol right in the hole." Ozzie bit his lip and made a face but didn't yell. He rolled to his right side. "Now in the back." The exit wound wasn't big, as I'd expected it to be from watching crime shows. Blood was oozing, not spurting. I think that meant no arteries were punctured. I poured the whole bottle in and he groaned. "Stitches," he muttered between clenched teeth.

I'd seen dozens of doctor shows. Grandma had shown me how to sew up a hole in my lucky running socks. Same thing, only it was human flesh. Ozzie's. I wiped my forehead. I was sweating as much as he was. I pinched the skin together and poked the needle through it, pulling the black thread. I could hear Ozzie's teeth grinding together. "Roll on your back," I said. I stitched the front hole, just below his shoulder. Ozzie closed his eyes and breathed deeply. It was just sewing.

"Bandages," he said, and I taped gauze to the front and back.

When I'd finished, I went to the little sink. I looked in the mirror to see a smear of blood on my forehead. I splashed water on my face and washed the blood off my hands. I'd done this before. I said over my shoulder, "Is this your vacation home?"

I turned around. Ozzie was snoring quietly. I slumped into the armchair and slept. Not even my bruises and aches could keep me awake.

అలఅలఅల

When I woke up, I went to the metal door and peered out. It was daylight. Ozzie was still asleep. He half woke up as I carefully washed the wound and changed the bandages. I took two ibuprofens. I hailed a cab on Twelfth Avenue and went to the Forty-Seventh Street YMCA to work out, trying to push through the pain. In the shower, I gently washed the black-and-blue bruises on my shoulder and my stomach. Then I shopped for food, some bottled water, and a new phone. I discovered while I was out that a whole day had passed. I called Mrs. Krasny to tell her I was visiting friends. I got some thrift store clothes for me.

When I got back to the storage unit, Ozzie was sitting up on the cot. The bloody sheets and blanket were on the floor.

"Feeling better?"

Ozzie nodded, raising his arm and wincing. "I am. Thank you."

"You're welcome. Do you have clean bedding? Another mattress?"

Ozzie smiled. "I'll call room service." He patted the cot next to him. "Now tell me why people want to kill you."

I told Ozzie almost everything: the Russians, the ledger, the missing money, the murder of my grandparents. Except I don't know who killed them. Maybe dead Sergei?

"Sergei and those fake cops, they're just tools. Somebody else sent them after you." Ozzie said. "They think you know something."

"But I don't know anything!" I almost shouted.

My heart hurt. A memory of the sharp things came then faded. They'd been a way of feeling sorry for myself. I missed Grandma and Grandpa. I had heard them, but I hadn't let myself feel them. But I wasn't sad. I was mad. I got up and paced back and forth.

Ozzie looked up at me. "There's something else."

There was Two-Ray. I told Ozzie about CC. Ozzie got a newspaper from under the cot. The one with my picture. "That's you."

I stared at him. "How did you know?"

"Your jeans with the holes. Your boots. The way you were standing, ready to fight."

I said to myself, *the way you taught me. The way that saved my life, that twice stopped bad people from killing me.* He took a laptop out from under the cot and plugged his phone into it. News feeds reported the gunfire on Elizabeth Avenue. Another article: a shootout at a Russian nightclub in Brooklyn. Police arrived to find an abandoned truck full of fake designer clothes, shoes, and handbags. *Uncle Teddy's merchandise,* I thought.

The hard faces of Uncle Teddy's men went through my head. It could have been any of them. For all the talk of family, loyalty, and brotherhood, if someone saw a weakness at the top, they'd take advantage. That's how Uncle Teddy came to be the head of the *orhanizatsiyi*. Gangster Darwinism.

I flopped down on the bed. A part of me, the seventeen-year-old girl, was disappearing. I used to have second thoughts about most decisions: catch up to Brianna early in the race, or wait till the last mile? Do my homework now, or wait until Grandma yelled at me? Teenage Deb had gone away, along with the shards of glass in my head. I'd made my brain too tough for them to penetrate—hard like a rock, focused, a *vovchytsya* standing on a snow-covered hill. Whoever was after me, whoever thought I was weak, a victim of a drug overdose or collateral damage in a street shooting, he was in for a surprise. I was after him, the faceless person on the other side of the wooden fence, keeping up with me as I ran. I was running toward the end of the fence now.

Tears came unbidden, soaking the pillow. A little of the old, sad, second-place Deb. If I were still mourning, I could save it for later. For afterward.

I felt the cot move as Ozzie sat down next to me. His hand was on my back, rubbing it. I sat up and pulled him to me. But I touched his arm, and he pulled away. "Ouch."

"Oops. Sorry."

Ozzie laughed then leaned forward and hugged me. He squeezed my shoulder where I'd been slammed with the blackjack, and it was my turn. "Ow!" We both laughed.

I felt something new. Maybe it was desire. I pulled him toward me. I wanted him. But Ozzie groaned again and put his hand to the bullet wound on his shoulder.

"Another reason not to do this," he said.

"I'm almost seventeen and a half," I replied, knowing what he meant.

"That's reason one," he said.

We lay down squeezed together on the cot. I still wanted him. But I wanted to sleep more. I guess Ozzie did too.

かかか

We stayed in the container-apartment for two more days to heal. We slept all huddled together on the tiny cot, but we didn't—what do I call it? Make love? Have sex? Anyway, we didn't do it.

We went out to eat and take walks down by the river. I told Ozzie about me: about growing up with my grandparents, about running, about the night my grandparents were murdered. Ozzie told me about himself: growing up in a Ukrainian family in Israel, joining the army, where he learned Krav Maga, the fighting style he taught me. He came to the United States and worked in various jobs. He'd stopped a robbery at a convenience store and somehow became the neighborhood cop.

"I'd take walks around at night."

"That's how we met," I said.

Ozzie's phone buzzed, and he answered it. After a few seconds, his face changed. "I'll be there," he said, and clicked off. "I've got to go."

"What's up?" I asked.

Ozzie looked away then back at me. "A friend said a Russian in the neighborhood was asking about me. About you."

It wasn't over. It wasn't going to be over until I did something. "Can I help?"

He shook his head. "Get your things."

"Take me to Penn," I said. "I have to go home."

Ozzie locked up the storage unit. We got in the van and drove away.

CHAPTER

I walked from the El stop on Ocean Parkway to the vacant house and found the Buick in the rear yard, battered and banged up. I knew how it felt. It started on the first try. I drove back to Brighton 2nd Street, parking it in the driveway. I stood on the front porch and yelled to the neighborhood, "I'm back. Deborah Sokolov is home."

"Hi Grandma, Grandpa. I'm home," I said to their empty bedroom. Downstairs, I went into Grandpa's office, cleaned and reloaded the Nagant, and put it on the desk. I sat in Grandpa's squeaky chair and watched out the window. Five minutes later, I realized: I had to hunt.

❧ ❧ ❧

I parked in the lot behind East-West Imports. Hugging the brick wall and looking out for security cameras, I made my way to the basement shooting range. Taking Grandpa's keys out of my pocket, I opened the door and punched in the alarm key code to disarm it.

The room still smelled of gunpowder and gun oil. I pushed away the memories that rose up like mushrooms growing in darkness. With my phone's flashlight, I found my way up the inside stairs to the main warehouse. It was quiet and dark. The garage for the *orhanizatsiyi's* fleet was at the far end of the main floor.

I used to play hide and seek with Grandpa in here; it felt like when I had sat with Mr. Krasny looking at the photos of a young child that everybody said was me. Like somebody else's memory. Boxes and crates stretched into the darkness. I opened the glass-windowed door to the garage and shined my light on them. There were four vehicles, all SUVs, all black. I checked the fenders for dents, the windshields and passenger seats for marks. Nothing. The SUV in the video could belong to the Russians.

Cars pulled up outside. I gripped the Nagant in my jacket but instantly realized it was a stupid idea. Maybe I wanted to go down in flames, but not until I found out what I needed to know. I heard the beep-beep of a truck backing up, and I hurried out of the garage into the warehouse.

The big metal door rattled open. I peeked over the top of a crate and saw a forklift coming into the warehouse. The crates I was hiding behind might be the ones they were coming for.

A wooden panel in the back corner of the warehouse had been my hide-and-seek hideaway. It was tucked under a long workbench to cover a hole in the wall with access to pipes and plumbing. Grandpa knew about it but pretended he didn't so I could jump out and surprise him.

I heard voices. "*Kakiye?*"

"*Vse troye za dver'yu.*" Russian, not Ukrainian. The forklift rolled into the warehouse.

The wooden panel screeched when I pulled on it. Maybe

the forklift made too much noise for them to hear it. Or maybe not. I squeezed inside, realizing my seventeen-year-old body was bigger than my eight-year-old one. I moved the panel to cover the hole, the pipes jamming against my back. Footsteps came closer. My right foot couldn't fit in the access and panel stuck out. The warehouse lights were off, the workbench hid the access, so they wouldn't notice. Maybe.

"Do you know where to go?" Voly's voice.

"The warehouse at Teterboro." No one I knew. A Russian.

"The plane leaves at three thirty, so you'll have to hurry."

"I have a watch. *Ya mogu skazat´ vremya.*"

Voly and the other guy walked past my hideaway, and I tried to ignore the pain in my back from the pipes. I could see the circles of light from their flashlights. I had a wild thought about climbing out of my hidey-hole and asking Voly what was up. I thought better of it. I didn't know what the Russian might do.

Someone yelled from near the door, "All set." After a minute, the metal door rolled down. I crawled out from under the bench and ran to the grime-coated window to look. The truck was pulling away, and Voly stood beside a black SUV, talking on his phone. After a minute, he opened the car door.

The passenger seat had a rip across the upholstery with some foam sticking out. There was a dent in the fender.

I took out my phone and scrolled through pictures. There it was: 05-14, 11:51 p.m. The black SUV on Ocean, a dented fender, and the blurry line across the passenger seat.

When I was little, Voly used to walk with me to Century playground and catch me at the bottom of the slide. When I was eight or nine, Voly taught me how to ride my first bicycle, held me and bandaged my knee when I fell off. Voly took me to the library and read the *Daily News* while I did my homework. Voly took me to see *Frozen*, where he kept looking at his watch. Voly, with tears running down his face, grabbed me and held me on that night, his tears hitting my cheeks, his big arms keeping me from running to the body bags that held my dead grandparents.

Voly killed them. He killed my grandparents to cover up the thefts. He sent the killer who came to my apartment, and the ones who chased me in the car.

I stared out the dirty window. Tears filled my eyes. I had to go home, to think. On my way to the door, I stubbed my foot on a cardboard box. Two cardboard boxes, taped shut. I peeled off the tape.

Inside were dozens of black plastic DVD boxes. *Daddy's Home*, *Kids at Play*, *Teacher's Pet*. I slammed the flap shut. As I stood up, the light from my phone revealed handwritten letters on the box flap: Rcvd. VB. Volodymyr Boroshnik.

Outside, in the gravel parking lot, I inhaled the salt and fish odor of the East River, saw a boat heading out and the lights from the city shining, twinkling, as if from another world. I heard the waves from the passing boat slapping on the shore.

I sat on a wooden railroad tie. Waves of sadness and self-pity rose in me. I pushed them away.

Some people need killing, Olek had said. Voly needed killing.

I drove home and parked in the driveway, holding the Nagant as I got out. I went through the back door and into the kitchen. Something hit me from behind, and pain rocketed through my head. I felt myself falling, and then nothing.

PART THREE: NOW

CHAPTER

I stood up, and Fatty pointed his Glock at my face. As I expected. With my hands still bound, I grabbed his wrist and shoved the gun to one side. Two muffled shots clanged off the post behind me. I bent my elbows, clenched my fists, and punched him five times in the face, as quickly as Ozzie. Fatty, already bleeding, rushed at me. I stepped to the side and shoved him, hard, forward and into the bench behind me.

Fatty fell to the ground, and something clattered to the wooden floor from his coat pocket.

Grandpa's Nagant.

I grabbed it and popped the cylinder. Loaded. I kicked Fatty in the head three times, almost as fast as Ozzie. The Nagant in my hand, I went to get the Glock, but my wrists were bound and I couldn't hold both guns. I heard footsteps. Armin was coming back. He shot at me, aiming too high.

I turned and ran out of the shelter and onto the sand, heading for the Steeplechase Pier. The moon was down, and it was dark, but there were lights on the pier. I heard a bullet whiz by me. A half-second later, I heard the shot.

I ran. I ran and ran. Another mile to go, I could find a place under the pier. Make them come and get me.

I ran, my heart pumping fast and strong, my legs like pistons, like coach Robbins told me would happen when I was in the zone. I looked straight ahead, seeing the pier come closer, and I knew that if I looked to the side, I'd see a faint echo of the wooden fence of my dreams, with the other head bobbing up and down, running. But I was running faster this time, faster and smarter, and the unknown runner was not going to beat me, not this time. I am *vovchytsya*.

Halfway to the pier, I slowed down and looked over my shoulder. Another car, a dark SUV, had pulled up in front of the café. Voly coming to finish what he'd started when he'd killed Grandma and Grandpa. Armin and Fatty got in, and the car squealed away, heading down the boardwalk toward the pier. Fast as I was running, the car would get there first.

How many rounds, Deborah?

Seven, Grandpa.

What is the maximum range for accuracy?

Twenty-five to fifty feet, if I'm good.

A chuckle. If *you are that good.*

I am that good, Didus.

The car stopped at the pier, and the car doors opened. When the dome light came on, I crouched in the sand, aimed, and fired one shot. No chance of hitting anything at two hundred yards, but it might slow them down. The doors slammed shut, and the car moved ahead to the other side of the pier, not visible. A silenced shot hit the sand where I'd been, and I started running again. I wasn't even winded.

Six shots left, Deborah.

I know, Grandpa. I know.

Under the pier in the darkness. Sand in my boots. Long Island Sound wavelets splashed against the wooden posts.

I ran down the sloping wet sand toward the water where the pier was higher above me, giving me more room to move in the shadows underneath. I found a jagged piece of metal sticking out of a piling and rubbed the plastic tie binding my wrists on it, trying to cut it. I heard shouts in Russian I didn't understand, and I hurried. Finally, the tie fell from my wrists, and I had a jagged, bleeding cut on my right wrist. I dipped it into the salty water of the sound, the Nagant in my left hand. *They're coming to look for me, in the darkness. They think I'll be hiding. Vovchytsya does not hide; she hunts.*

"*Ostavaytes' zdes'!*" someone yelled. Russian. No clue, but I guessed it was instructions. I looked back to see the two Russians a hundred feet away walking down the beach on either side of the pier. Its lights were just bright enough to see the guns in their hands, noise suppressors at the muzzle. Above me, I heard footsteps on the pier. Voly.

I waded into the water. To my right was a small rock jetty. If I could get there, they'd have to come out in the open. But it was thirty feet away, and I'd be exposed to Voly on the pier above.

I crouched down, stepped out from under the pier, and looked up to see a silhouette on the pier above cradling a long gun. Voly might have to take five shots, but he only needed one. He looked down, aimed, and fired just as I ran back under the pier. He was firing auto: five, then ten, rounds kicking up sand behind me.

The Russians hurried down the beach on either side of the pier, heading to me. I had nowhere to go. One of them yelled at Voly on the pier, "Stop shooting!"

Advantage: I could see them, but they couldn't see me.

Disadvantages: two of them, one of me, plus Voly above with a long gun, and they had umpteen rounds. I had six.

The fat Russian, about twenty yards away, pulled out a flashlight and shone it right on me. I ducked back, hearing two more silenced shots, one smacking the piling above my head. Using the pilings as cover, I ran deeper under the pier into the water. I was up to my ankles behind a piling.

Fatty stepped into the darkness under the pier, shining his flashlight around. I raised the Nagant.

Too far away yet, Deborah.

I know, Grandpa.

Fatty moved deeper under the pier, waving his flashlight. I waded slowly out of the water toward him, keeping pilings between us. I was maybe twenty feet away when a wave lapped up against a piling, splashing behind me. Fatty swung the flashlight, and I was in its glare. I fired the Nagant once, aiming just above the flashlight and to the left.

"Uhh," he said and fell facedown to the sand. A wavelet washed over him. I waded toward him, staying under cover of the pier. I wanted his pistol. On the sand was Voly's shadow above me with the long gun. No way.

"Dimitri! Did you get her?" Armin's voice called from somewhere behind me. I went deeper into the water, up to my knees, crouching as a flashlight beam swung by and lit up the dead Russian who used to be Dimitri.

"*Govno!*" Armin swore, probably something like hell, or damn, or shit.

How many rounds left?

Five, Grandpa.

Armin was just about opposite me, but the light from the pier kept him from seeing me as I crouched down with the Nagant in my right hand. He was smarter than Dimitri, turning off his flashlight, ducking behind a piling, and firing a shot or two into the darkness to keep me frosty. Above me I heard Voly's footsteps running back to the boardwalk. Trying to get away or get more ammo?

"Are you afraid, Sokolov? Are you nervous?" Armin said in his high-pitched voice. He wanted me to answer so he could locate me, but I'd seen that movie. Instead, I crouched and duckwalked backward behind another piling. Now I was to his left, and he stuck his head out from behind the piling, his head swiveling, his eyes still adjusting to the dark.

Too far away, Deborah.

I backed away quietly, heading to deeper water. My heel hit a piece of driftwood, and it scraped the sand. Armin fired but missed, hitting a wooden brace next to my head. He was good. A she-wolf is better.

As I slid to the left, my foot stepped on something. In the shallow water was a tiny seashell, a sand dollar. I remembered the one in my cigar box. I bent down, picked it up, and threw it to my right. It hit a wooden brace and went into the water. Armin spun in the sand and fired three shots at the sound. He was turned away, toward the water, peering into it to see if he'd got me. I stepped out, aimed at the back of his neck with the Nagant, fired once. He dropped like a suit falling off a hanger and splashed into the shallow water.

Four rounds left.

Now for Voly. I didn't see his silhouette on the sand. I risked a glance up at the pier. I hadn't heard a car drive off. Crouching down, I moved slowly toward the boardwalk, sticking close to the pilings in the shadows. Voly was still here. Waiting for me. I was coming.

I felt a cold hard something on the back of my neck. I spun aside and whirled, ready to grab it but got hit hard on the side of my head. I fell, and a rough hand yanked the Nagant from my grip. I rolled over and looked up.

Not Voly. Not Voly but Olek, standing a step away, the Kalashnikov aimed at me.

Of course it hadn't been Voly. I should have trusted my heart instead of my stupid brain filled with shrapnel, old pain, and revenge. *Vovchytsya* was hunting the wrong prey. I was second-place Deborah again, running along the fence, but the fence ended and then it was Olek, not Voly, waiting for me.

"You killed my grandparents," I said.

Olek nodded, trying to look sad. "I am so sorry for that. It was an accident."

I spit. "An accident! You went there to kill them!" I started to get up, but Olek gestured with the Kalashnikov.

Olek shook his head. "No, it wasn't like that. Teo was angry about the missing money. I went there to persuade Viktor to wait, to take another look at the books. He was a stubborn man, your grandfather. We argued. Nadiya attacked me with a kitchen knife." He rolled up his sleeve to reveal a three-inch scar on his forearm and smiled at the memory. "I think you have some of her in you as well."

"You killed my grandparents," I said again. "You sent those Russians to kill me. Because you're a coward."

Olek yelled, "You should have stayed away. I warned you—"

"By killing my cat? What a brave man you are, Olek."

He slammed me in the side of my head with the gun barrel. I guess I struck a nerve. "You know what's funny? I didn't even know it was you."

Olek shrugged. "It doesn't matter now, Deborah."

"You sent people to kill me because you're a coward. You hid stealing from your father, from the *orhanizatsiyi*. Because you're a coward."

Olek gestured with the Kalashnikov. "Get up."

"If you shoot me, it'll point to you," I said, feeling a bit desperate and not very she-wolfish right now.

"It's time," he said. He pulled me to my feet, and I looked around. "I am not a monster," the monster said. "I don't want you to suffer. You will be unconscious when you drown."

The boardwalk was deserted. There was the Café Volna, closed and dark. The moon was sinking behind the pier. The beach, empty, stretched out to the slow surge of waves lapping at the sand.

A car pulled up on the boardwalk behind me. A door slammed. Olek took a step back, aiming the Kalashnikov into the darkness. "I can shoot you and him in a half-second," he said by way of warning. A tall figure walked down the sand toward us. It was Voly.

Olek was surprised and unhappy. "What are you doing here, Volodymyr?"

Voly held up his cell phone. "Tracking your phone. Teodor asked me to keep an eye on Deborah. What are you doing, Olek?" he asked. "And don't point that at me," he added.

Olek put the long gun down, leaning it against a piling. "Deborah killed Dimitri and Armin. Because they killed Viktor and Nadiya." Olek licked his thin lips. "It was the Russians." Nervous was good, I thought.

"You killed Viktor and Nadiya, asshole," I said. Voly was here. He could help, he could stop Olek. I got to my knees, not caring. "He's been cheating Uncle Teddy and making deals behind his back with those guys. Olek is planning to get Uncle Teddy out of the way—probably kill him—and take over."

Voly looked at me, at the Russians, then at Olek. Then at me again. "This is a matter for Teodor," he said.

"This is with my father's approval," Olek replied.

Voly took out his cell phone. "We have rules, Olek. This is a matter for the *orhanizatsiyi*. Deborah is family."

Olek pulled the Nagant from his pocket and shot Voly twice in the chest. He fell to the sand. "See what you've done, Deborah? You've killed my most loyal man." Olek sighed. "Now I'll have to put your grandfather's revolver in your pocket for when they find you."

Olek grabbed my arm and marched to the water with the Nagant in my back. He held my arm tightly as we stepped forward into the still-shallow water.

Out of the corner of my eye, I saw him take something out of his shirt pocket. A syringe. "Another few moments, Deborah," he said. "The tide will take you, but we have to go deeper."

My foot stepped on something that hurt, and I stumbled. It was a stone under the water. In a half-second, the wolf came back. I could see its eyes glowing in the dark, staring at me. I fell to my knees, making Olek lose his grip on my arm, and grabbed the rock.

Before I could react, he stuck the syringe into my neck behind my ear. I yanked myself back. A little of whatever it was got into my veins, and it stung for a minute. Then pleasure, like good dope, came over me in waves.

As Olek leaned over to push the syringe deeper, I

grabbed his hand holding the syringe, leapt up, and swung the rock at him. I hit Olek in the face then pulled the Nagant to me, twisting his hand. He yelled, and in the dim light I saw blood coming from his nose. I moved inside his gun arm as he fired, and the shot went wide. I kicked him in the knee. As he lost his balance, I hit him again with the rock in his throat, like Ozzie had showed me. I grabbed the Nagant, and he let go of it, grabbing his neck and gasping. I turned and pushed my way through the waist-high water. I looked behind me. Olek fell then got up and ran back up to the beach. He was going for the Kalashnikov.

I know, Grandpa. Two shots left.

I headed back to the pier, pushing through the water, falling to my knees more than once, keeping my right hand with the Nagant above it as best as I could. The drug slowed me down a little, but I didn't care. I was not angry or scared or helpless. I slowed for a second and looked across the beach. I thought about running the mile back to the boardwalk, getting to Grandpa's Buick, and driving off. Olek couldn't catch me. But a she-wolf doesn't run away.

I looked behind me to see Olek climbing up to the pier, looking for me, the Kalashnikov in his hand. I turned and half-walked, half-swam under the pier. Olek saw me and fired.

I ducked through the pilings and got to the other side of the pier. I ran up the beach, staying in the shadows, to get behind him. Olek was still looking toward the other side of the pier, thinking I would try to run back to the boardwalk and the cars.

I climbed over the railing and got onto the pier. Olek was forty feet away, still looking down at the sand. He turned and saw me, aimed, and fired while backing away. A round clanged into the steel railing; another dug a hole in the pier to my left. He backed into one of the benches on the pier and stumbled. Two shots went into the air. I held the Nagant down at my side.

The Kalashnikov has a thirty-round magazine. How many has he left?

I don't care, Grandpa.

I was ten feet away from Olek when he aimed the Kalashnikov at me and squeezed the trigger. Click! Click! He threw the rifle at me. It clattered on the deck. He turned and ran down the pier toward the ocean. He had nowhere to go. I kept walking toward him, the gun at my side, one round left.

Olek stopped, turned, and raised his hands, half-smiling. "You are good, Deborah. Better than anyone imagined." He rubbed his throat where I'd hit him. "You have some of Viktor in you."

I came closer, leveling the Nagant at his chest. "You killed Voly. Because you're a coward."

Maybe the tears in my eyes made me lose focus. Maybe the she-wolf looked the other way for a split second. Olek leapt at me and shoved my gun hand to one side. He slammed his fist into my face, and I was just able to move to the side, minimizing the blow. I saw stars, but not in the sky. He reached for the Nagant, and I grabbed his wrist, pulled him to me, and kneed him in the balls.

Olek bent over with a groan that sounded like, "You whore!" I raised my knee into his face. A crack! told me I might have broken his shark fin nose. He grabbed me around the waist, and I stepped backward quickly. He lost his balance. He took another swing at me, aiming for my stomach.

I stepped into the punch before his arm was extended, blunting the force. It still hurt.

Olek again reached for my gun, and I slammed it down on his arm, then grabbed him and pulled him forward, stepping to the side. He fell face-first on the pier. I leaned down, grabbed his hair, and slammed his head into the wooden deck. I moved back, breathing hard.

Olek rolled over onto his back. He tried to sit up but fell back, groaning. Blood flowed from his nose and down his cheeks. Through bloodied lips, he rasped, "I give up. Call Teo. Call the cops. I don't care." He smiled his thin, gap-toothed smile.

I stood over him for a second then knelt onto his chest. He moaned, "Get off me!"

"Some people need killing," I said, and put the Nagant under his chin.

One shot left.

"It's all I need, Grandpa," I said out loud to the night. I pulled the trigger.

I didn't puke.

AUTHOR'S NOTE

Dear reader,

Thanks for reading She-Wolf. If you enjoyed it (even if you didn't!), I'd really appreciate a short review on your favorite online retail bookseller site.

I've got two books you might also be interested in: **Operation Overlord**, a middle grade historical fiction about World War II; and **Losing Normal**, an award-winning young adult novel about a boy on the autism spectrum who winds up saving us all.

You can download samples from my website: http://www.francismoss.com/books, plus I have included brief samples on the following pages.

I'd love to hear from you. You can email me at francismossbooks@gmail.com, or visit my blog at https://www.francismoss.com to see what I'm up to.

Thanks, and all the best,

ABOUT THE AUTHOR

Francis Moss has written and story-edited hundreds of hours of scripts on many of the top animated shows of the 90s and 00s, including *She-Ra, Princess of Power, Iron Man, Ducktales,* and a four-year stint on *Teenage Mutant Ninja Turtles.* One of his TMNT scripts, "The Fifth Turtle," was the top-rated episode of all the 193 shows in a fan poll on IGN.COM.

He's the co-author of three middle-grade non-fiction books: *Internet For Kids, Make Your Own Web Page,* and *How To Find (Almost) Anything On The Internet,* and sole author of *The Rosenberg Espionage Case.*

EXCERPTS FROM
FRANCIS MOSS' BOOKS

LOSING NORMAL

The bell rang at 8:13 AM, and kids began running down the hall to their classes. I started walking to the main hall when Emilio touched my shoulder. I stopped. "Let's wait," he said. A minute and ten seconds later, the hallway emptied and grew quiet. Emilio went ahead and looked around the corner. He waved his hand, which means "come on. "

We walked down the white hallway, staying close to the wall of lockers. We had almost gotten to the door of the Resource Room when Chuck Schwartz, who is my enemy, stepped out of the stairwell. Emilio moved behind me. Chuck Schwartz smiled, but I have seen that smile before. He has a gap between his front teeth. He wore a black T-shirt with no sleeves.

"Hey, Ass-burger!" he said. He walked down the hall toward us, his black boots thumping on the floor. Chuck Schwartz rammed his shoulder into me and smashed me sideways into the lockers. "Watch where you're going, Ass-burger." This was normal.

"I always watch where I'm going," I said, which was

stupid. Chuck Schwartz put his hand on my chest and shoved me against the lockers. Emilio backed away, but Chuck Schwartz reached out with his left arm and grabbed him by his shirt. "No, no. You're next. "We stood there for seven seconds. Chuck Schwartz stared at me, and I looked down at the floor, which is what I usually do.

Then I heard a deep voice: "What are you doing?" I looked up to see Mr. Crumley, an older man who volunteers in the library, behind Chuck Schwartz. He has a little white beard and always wears a green tweed jacket and a white shirt buttoned up to his neck.

He put his hand on Chuck Schwartz's shoulder, and Chuck Schwartz let go of us fast. "Just having a conversation, dude."

"Go. Now. Dude," Mr. Crumley said.

Chuck Schwartz headed down the hallway. He turned back and did that thing with his index and middle finger, pointing at his eyes, then at me and Emilio.

"Need a ride home today?" Mr. Crumley asked.

I looked down and shook my head, although I really like Mr. Crumley's red and white 1955 Chevrolet Bel-Air. Mom had asked him to bring me home a few times when she had to work late at the hospital.

"Thank you, sir," Emilio said.

Mr. Crumley nodded. "Are you all right, Alex?" he asked. I shrugged, which is my default answer. Mr. Crumley turned and walked down the hall. "You're late for class," he said over his shoulder.

A black big-screen monitor hung on the green wall in the Resource Room. This was not normal. Mr. Bates, who usually wore a white short-sleeved shirt and a bow tie, stood behind his desk, next to a blonde woman I'd never seen before. She was wearing a black pant suit and held a tablet computer.

The three other special kids were already there: Bobby turned his head from side to side, going "Woo, woo, woo." Fat Carlos had his head on his desk. The new girl, Sara, who has red hair, freckles, and green eyes, played a game on her phone. She had transferred from another school in the middle of the semester. She looked at me and nodded. "Hey, Rinato," she said.

I stood at the door until Mr. Bates motioned to me to sit down. Emilio went to his regular seat behind me.

Mr. Bates adjusted his glasses and turned to us. "Sara, put your phone away. Everyone, settle down, settle down." We mostly settled down.

Mr. Bates pointed to the monitor. "We've got something special today, class. The Calliope people have come up with a brand-new curriculum, just for us."

He nodded to the blonde woman. She stepped to the front of the class. "Hi. I'm Lucinda Clark and I'm in charge of new technologies at Calliope. Watch this short video; we'll talk about your experiences afterward." She pointed a remote control at the big screen. The man I had just seen on the big screen on Woodbine appeared on this screen, but now he wore long khaki pants and a blue shirt.

"My name is William Locke. You've probably seen me on TV," he chuckled. The blonde and Mr. Bates laughed, but no one else did. "When I was growing up, I had learning problems and behavior problems in school, like some of you. I wish I could have had the program we're about to show you." He smiled. "All right, let's give it a look."

A logo of a yellow sun held in bright blue hands and the word 'Calliope' appeared on the screen. A woman's voice said: "Welcome to Calliope Education! We know that these years of rapid changes in your growing minds and bodies can be challenging and even a little scary at times. This program is designed to help you meet these challenges."

My hands started flapping on my legs. The room disappeared and all I could see were the swarms of fruit flies, spinning like a whirlpool, stretching from the screen, coming at me. My head started to hurt. I closed my eyes and covered my ears with my hands, but I could still see the fruit flies in my head. I tried to push them away.

I heard a crash and opened my eyes. Fat Carlos was sprawled on the floor. Emilio stared at the screen, a little smile on his face. Bobby banged his head on his desk, screaming "Woo! Woo! Woo!" Sara squinted and held her ears. Fat Carlos got up off the floor, then ran out the door, screaming, "Bad! Bad!" Mr. Bates waved his hands in the air, like one of those inflatable things they have in front of stores. My legs started bouncing up and down, my hands flapping. The picture on the screen was a fountain of red and black, filling the room and filling my head, pushing everything else out. My name is Alex. My name is Alex.

I pushed back, there was a loud crash, and everything went away. I opened my eyes and found I was lying on the floor. Sara knelt beside me, holding her head. "Ow! Ow!"

The day before my dad left for Afghanistan, we went to a seafood restaurant on the coast highway. I had a hamburger. When we left the restaurant, the fog had come in, making halos around the lights. I watched out the rear window of our Volvo as we drove away. The lights grew dimmer and dimmer, then disappeared into the gray fog. For three seconds, I remembered something red and black that came from the screen, but then it faded into gray.

I had a headache. I sat up and saw that the monitor was shattered. Pieces of the screen's black glass covered the floor. The blonde woman looked at her tablet, and then she looked at me.

A sample from Francis Moss's
latest MG novel

OPERATION OVERLORD

The teams formed up, one at each end of the pitch. Lymes blew his whistle, and the game began. Stumpy forwarded the ball to Tommy. He kicked it downfield toward the opposing goal, called "Worms." Felton, a lad from College, snatched it up and ran down the field to the goal.

Tommy called out the foul: "Handiwork! Handiwork!" He stepped in front of Felton to block his progress. "Taking more than three steps whilst holding the ball is against the rules."

Tommy looked to Housemaster Lymes for support, but the man's attention was elsewhere. Every boy on both sides stared up into the thinning clouds, recognizing the sound of an aircraft engine. Reynolds, the house kicker, shouted, "Doodlebug!" and started running across the field toward the gate. The town air raid sirens started wailing.

The engine noise grew louder. Then the craft descended below the clouds: not a V-1 aerial bomb or the doodlebug Reynolds thought it was, but a German fighter plane. It was speckled with green, brown, and olive camouflage paint, the swastika clearly visible on the wings and tail. It was coming in low, not two hundred yards away, and heading for the muddy field. Its engine had stopped, and the propeller fluttered. Its fuselage was peppered with bullet holes.

"Form up quickly!" the housemaster called. "Back to the College!"